WALKER OF THE SECRET SERVICE

Melville Davisson Post. Frontispiece by John Betancourt.

WALKER OF THE SECRET SERVICE

MELVILLE DAVISSON POST

WILDSIDE PRESS

INTRODUCTION

Melville Davisson Post (1869– 1930) was an American author, born in Harrison County, West Virginia. Although his name is not immediately familiar to those outside of specialist circles, many of his short story collections are still in print, and many anthologies of detective fiction include works by him. Post's best-known character is the mystery solving, justice dispensing West Virginian backwoodsman, Uncle Abner. There are 22 Uncle Abner tales, written between 1911 and 1928, have been called some of "the finest mysteries ever written" by critic Joseph Bottum.

Post's other recurring characters include the lawyers Randolph Mason and Colonel Braxton, and the detectives Sir Henry Marquis and Monsieur Jonquelle. In all, he produced about 230 titles, including several non-crime novels.

—Karl Wurf
Rockville, Maryland

CHAPTER I

THE OUTLAW

Near the entrance of the great circus tent there was a little man in a canvas chair. He sat at the end of the long alley, which was hung with painted signs.

Nothing had escaped me.

I had no money to see any wonder, and so had to be content with what was displayed outside. It was early in the morning. The grass before the tents had not yet been trodden down; few persons were about, and I had the marvels of this fantastic alley to myself.

I had advanced slowly along every foot of it, and now I stood just beyond the roped-off entrance to the big tent, and the little man in the canvas chair.

There was something in the appearance of this man that drew my eye. He sat in the chair as though every muscle were relaxed, his eyes closed, his head drooping. Now and then he put up his hand and pressed the fingers over his face. It seemed a habit, as though his face had the sensation of being swollen.

No one disturbed him. He had been there for some time. I had noticed him at the end of the alley when I arrived, precisely in this posture, as of one worn out with some exertion.

I was looking at him as I had looked at the painted signs when the canvas of the big tent was thrust up and a man came out. He was a big young man in the overalls of a mechanic and he had some device in his hand like a dome-shaped metallic box.

He went directly to the man in the canvas chair.

"Mooney," he said, "there's something wrong with this damned thing; make it go."

The little man opened his eyes without moving a muscle of his body. Then he put out his hand, took the metallic device, rested it on his knee, flicked a penknife out of his waistcoat pocket, and with a screw-driver blade took a plate off at the bottom of the thing. Then he adjusted something deftly inside, replaced the plate and returned the device to the mechanic.

It had taken only a moment; his fingers had moved with the precision of a pianist, and he had scarcely changed his position.

I had been greatly interested and had drawn a little closer. And when I looked up, the eyes of the big mechanic were on me; he had a hard, determined face and a sharp, piercing eye. I felt that he easily summed me up and had the measure of me. The little man in the canvas chair spoke as the mechanic turned away.

"White," he said, "who's it goin' to be?"

"I don't know yet," replied the mechanic. "I'll look 'em over."

Then he disappeared under the circus tent.

I realized now that I was very close to the man in the canvas chair, and I stepped back across the green alley. A little group of tent hands were speaking as I came up.

"I wonder why they stick," one of them was saying. "They can't get much out of the boss for fixing these jimcracks.... The big one's an expert mechanic and the dope Jimmy's a wizard."

It was late in the afternoon when I again saw the big mechanic.

The crowd from the circus was scattering. I had nowhere to go and was standing idly in the road when the man came up. He looked me over very carefully.

"Young fellow," he said, "you don't seem to be in much of a hurry; perhaps you could take a note over to the Red Sign Bar."

I explained that I was a stranger in the town, but he pointed out very definitely how I could find the way.

"You will go into the bar," he said, "and go straight through to the back room. There you will find the tired man who fixed the dynamo. Give him this note."

He handed me a blank envelope sealed, and half a dollar. I needed the half dollar, for I was hungry. I had not a cent in the world and I had walked that afternoon ten miles into the town.

It was not possible to mistake the directions. I followed the road the circus wagons had made from the meadow where the tents were stretched, to the town. One could not miss the main street through it.

Presently I found the Red Sign Bar. The bar was crowded, so my passage was not marked. I opened the door at the end and went into a room.

Immediately the man sitting at the table sprang up.

On the table before him were a number of railroad folders and a map, and he was making some calculations on a blank sheet of paper.

He was the same man whom I had seen in the canvas chair in the alley of side shows before the big tent of the circus. But he was visibly changed. He was like a cat, incredibly active. His hands were in his pockets and he did not move after he was on his feet.

I closed the door and, going forward, put the envelope on the table.

"A gentleman out at the circus," I said, "sent you this letter."

He sat down with the same soft, quick feline motion, tore the envelope open with his finger and read the contents. But I had the feeling that while his eyes were on the paper they were also very carefully on me. Then suddenly he spoke.

"Do you know why White picked you?"

"Picked me for what?" I said.

He folded the paper over his finger and, reaching across the table, showed me the lower half of what the note contained.

It was written in pencil in a large clear hand:

> The same baby that we spotted at the Junction goes to the tank at 10:15 to-night. She always takes a drink at this trough. I think there is money in her clothes, and here's a fellow to help.
>
> White.

He whisked the note back into his pocket.

"So you are going to help us," he said. "You look like a husky youngster."

I was completely puzzled, but, as you will presently realize, I was ready for almost any adventure. My first clash with organized society had left me bewildered, and ready for any revenge that might present itself.

The little nervous man, Mooney, regarded me searchingly for some moments before he spoke. Then he said:

"Damn the Mexican government! There is some of its money going south to-night. How would you like to have a piece of it?"

As I have said, I was ready for nearly any adventure, but especially an adventure directed against a government with which we had lately been at war, and which was still, one felt, a potential enemy.

I did not reply.

Mooney leaned back in his chair and regarded me for some time, his hand moving about his face.

"You will be a stranger here," he said, "and a reliable person or White would have passed you up. He has the eye of the devil for seeing through a man. Here's a dollar."

He took a paper dollar out of his waistcoat pocket and handed it to me.

"Do two things," he said, "and don't talk; go out and get something to eat and after that hunt up a piece of quarter-inch pipe about two feet long; slip it up your coat sleeve and be at the entrance of the big circus tent at eight o'clock."

I went out like a person who has suddenly fallen from the common-place world into some story of the *Arabian Nights*.

There was about me and over the world a haze of adventure. The details of this adventure were not clear, but it was one directed against the crooked Mexican government, and it involved a treasure like the treasure of the sunken Armadas.

It was the alluring stuff of the storybooks. I was ready for it with these strange adventurers.

This state of feeling requires a word here.

After my father's death, as I was now alone, I came down out of the great blue mountains to seek my fortune, as the storybooks say. I walked, and on the road I was overtaken by an adventure. Near a little village I passed one of those local trains, common to this country: an engine, one or two cars, and an old passenger coach. The highway passed close beside the track, and as I trudged along a fireman leaned out of the tender and called to me.

"Hey, Reuben," he said, "ring your bell when you pass."

I told him with some heat, that I would ring his neck if he came down out of his iron box, and I went on.

But the thing was not ended. The train presently pulled on and, as it passed, the fireman threw a lump of coal at me. I countered at him with a stone, that missed the tender and struck the passenger car behind it.

At the next village I was arrested and taken before a justice of the peace. There I was told that it was a felony, under the laws of the state, to throw a stone at a passenger train, and that the railroad intended to put me into the penitentiary.

"And what are you going to do with the fireman who threw a lump of coal at me?" I said.

"Nothing," replied the justice. "He didn't hit you."

"Then you'll not do anything with me," I said, and I rose.

The little office of the Justice was at the end of the village. A railroad detective sat beside me; the fireman who had made the charge lolled in the door.

It all happened in a moment.

I threw off the railroad detective who caught at my arm and as the big fireman swung around into the door I struck him as hard as I could in the chest. He went crashing down the steps. I jumped through the door and ran. The railroad detective followed me, firing his pistol. But he was no match for my youth across the fields, and he was soon out of sight.

I turned back the way I had come, crossed to another highway; and here on this afternoon I was. I did not know how far I had traveled and hardly the direction. You will see then how ready I was for any adventure—and especially if a railroad was included. It had become, by virtue of the injustice of this incident, an enemy open to revenge.

I had no trouble to find a dinner, but I found myself beset with difficulty about the piece of pipe. I tramped about the town during the afternoon, but I could think of no place where a piece of quarter-inch pipe could be obtained. It did not occur to me to go to a plumbing shop, and if I had thought of that I would not have known what excuse to make for my purchase. Besides, I had no money. You will remember that I was young and extremely hungry and the dollar and a half had disappeared in carrying out Mooney's first direction.

I thought I should have to give it up.

Finally in a blacksmith shop I found a rusted rod that had been part of a wagon brake. I asked the blacksmith to give it to me. Naturally, he wished to know what I was going to do with it, and for a moment I was in difficulty for an answer. Then I told him that they wanted such a piece of iron out at the circus, and had promised to give me a ticket in if I could find it. He laughed.

"I'm glad," he said, "that there's something else they want, if the elephant ain't thirsty."

He flung me the rod and wished that I might enjoy the circus.

I had it in my sleeve when White appeared in the grass alley before the circus entrance.

I got out of the crowd and followed him. It was now dark. We went around the big tent, through the stables for the horses, then struck out across the meadow in a direction opposite from the town.

I walked beside him with my piece of rod in my sleeve, very much as a child, it now seems to me, might set out on a fairy expedition with an all-abiding confidence in the resources of those conducting him, and with no clear idea of what he might come to, unconcerned and careless of events.

White had very few words during the long walk through the dark in the meadow.

"You are a husky youngster," he said. "You could shove along a bull wagon or I miss my guess."

He was correct in that estimate. I was a sturdy youngster, hardened by the out-of-doors. Physically I was developed, but I seemed in my conception of affairs to have been still a child, albeit approaching that stage of youth where, instantly, as by merely awaking in the morning, one becomes a man.

We came finally to the railroad track. There was a short switch with a little red house beside it. It was less a house than a sort of box with a low door. Leaning against this door, when we arrived, was Mooney.

He was smoking a cigarette; the tiny point of light had been visible to us as we approached.

"Young man," he said, "did you bring the piece of pipe?"

I drew the rod out of my sleeve and handed it to him. He struck a match and examined the door; there was a padlock on it. He thrust the rod through the bow of the padlock and with a quick twist broke it out of the lock. Inside was a hand car, and then it was that I realized why these men were concerned to have what they called a "husky" assistant.

It was with difficulty that we were able to get the car on the track. Finally it was accomplished and we started away in the darkness. I knew nothing about the operation of a hand car, but I was quickly shown. We set out in the direction which I took to be south of the town. White and I on opposite sides pumped the car and Mooney squatted on the platform. He had under him what looked like a feed sack, filled with something that had a considerable bulk. He carried also the iron rod in his hand, but it had served his purpose. At the first stream we crossed he tossed it into the water.

It was a piece of possible evidence and he did not wish it to be picked up along the track. True, it connected neither him nor White with the thing which we were undertaking, but perhaps I might be remembered by it, and it was this man's policy to leave no point at which any one could begin with his investigation.

We went on for some time into the night.

Once in a while we passed a house lighted in the distance, but no village and no dwelling near the track. There was hardly any sound except that of the car on the rails. I wondered at how still the world could be. For a long time we continued to move south, White and I at the pump handles of the car and Mooney, as I have said, squatted on the platform.

Suddenly in the silence he swore softly.

"What's the matter?" said White.

The little nervous man replied, drawling out the words.

"It's an ax," he said. "We ought to have an ax."

"That's easy," replied White. "We'll pull up at the next house and send our young friend to borrow one."

And they followed that plan. At a turn of the road we made out a house a few hundred yards above us on the slope of the hill. The car stopped and I went to borrow an ax.

I do not know how it happened that there was no dog about, for there are dogs at all these houses in the south. I looked outside, but there was no ax to be found. Then I looked in at the window.

There was a wood fire dying down in the fireplace, and a ladder leading to the loft. The person who lived there was evidently in his bed above. The man's coat and boots were on the floor by the ladder, and beside the chimney there were some tools—a mattock, a hoe, and the ax for which I was looking. It was a hinged window secured on the inside by a button. The ax was safe from any method that I knew, and I went back to the hand car.

I told the men what I had found.

Mooney got up from his sack on the platform.

"My son," he said, "I will show you something useful; let us go back for the ax."

As we went along he took a newspaper out of his pocket and dipped it in a ditch until it was thoroughly wet. When we reached the window he spread the wet paper against the glass and with the pressure of his hand broke the pane out.

The broken glass stuck to the paper and it made almost no sound.

Then he put his hand through and unbuttoned the latch, opened the window and climbed in noiselessly like a cat, got the ax and came out.

We were very near to our destination, it proved, and in half an hour we reached a water tank. It was near a little creek and in a strip of wood. I had judged that we were on our way to a water tank from the few lines Mooney had shown me, and what he had said. The money of the Mexican government would be on a train that would stop here for water, and, like the pirates of the Spanish Main, it was our affair to capture the treasure.

We stopped. Mooney got down and removed from the car a bundle upon which he had been sitting. White and I upended the hand car and sent it down the embankment into the thick bushes; then we moved around behind the water tank to prepare for the undertaking.

The night had long ceased to be dark. There was no moon, but the sky was sown with stars, and there was a sort of faint white light in the world. We could see distinctly what we were about, even in the thicket behind the water tank, shaded somewhat by the wood. Here Mooney untied his bundle.

It contained three suits of overalls such as are worn by railroad men, blue trousers and a sort of blue coat; they were not new. Mooney was too clever a person, as I came afterward to realize, to make his party conspicuous by any new article.

This was the disguise for our bodies. For head covering Mooney had three sugar sacks dyed black, with round holes for the eyes and mouth. These we pulled over our heads. He had also an ordinary burlap feed sack—the "loot sack," he called it.

Then he brought out the weapons.

He made a little speech about these weapons. They were the latest model of automatic pistols, each precisely like the others. He said it was a great mistake to go out with a different variety of weapons because in a protracted fight there could be no exchange of ammunition.

His voice drawled with nervous jerks at the end of it. He might have been lecturing to a Sunday school. He asked me if I understood the weapon. I did not understand it and said so.

"Well," he said, "it is simple enough. You have only to pull the trigger and keep on pulling it; whatever happens will be over by the time you get to the last cartridge. Don't worry about it, my son."

He added another direction:

"Turn the muzzle up when you shoot; it don't do any good to hit 'em."

He made a little ridiculous gesture.

"The maneuvers of train robbing," he said, "are directed against the mind."

Then he explained what each of us was to do.

White was to use the ax in order to break in the door of the express car. He, Mooney, would be the gunman, and it was my part in the business to stand on the platform between the express car and the next passenger coach to keep back the conductor or any one else who might attempt to go forward into the train.

They seemed to know precisely what the trainmen would do, and were prepared to meet it. Either the man called White had watched this train on some previous night or he had taken some other precaution to discover precisely what would happen when the train stopped at the tank, for they went into their parts when the event arrived precisely as though they had drilled for it and were entering at the cue of some director.

We were hidden in the bushes close beside the tank when the train rolled in.

To me it seemed immense, gigantic, in the darkness. The blinding headlight, the roar, and grating of the brakes seemed to make a bewildering confusion. I think I should not have moved from the bushes, in such confusion was I thrown, had I not been between the two men; and as it happened, I got up with them.

We waited until the engine had taken water and the conductor and porter had made their round of the train; then we slipped out of our hiding place as the train pulled out. We swung on to the rear platform of the express car precisely at the moment that the porter climbed on to the steps of the same platform at the other side.

Mooney jammed his gun into the man's face.

The porter nearly lost his hold on the rail of the car with terror.

"My God!" he muttered. "Don't shoot."

We must have presented every element of terror to him—the deadly weapons and the three looming figures in their black peaked caps.

"Keep still," said Mooney. "Do what you are told and you won't get hurt."

White tried the door to the express car; it was open. He pitched away the ax, seized the porter by the shoulders, and he and Mooney rushed the express car, using the body of the terrorized porter for a shield against any bullet that might be fired.

To their surprise they found the baggage master, mail clerk and express messenger all sitting on the floor eating lunch from dinner buckets.

There was no resistance.

They all threw up their hands almost with a single motion.

"Which is the express messenger?" said Mooney.

"I am," replied one of the men.

"I want what you have in the way box," he said.

The messenger denied having anything.

"Give me your key and I will find out."

Mooney went about the thing with deliberation. He unlocked the box, took out all packages, and put them in his loot sack. Then he left White to stand guard over the men while he took the mail clerk into the mail car to see what he could get there.

All this time I was standing at my post between the two cars looking through the glass door into the faces of the passengers. I could see the faces of the men before me clearly, for I was looking from the dark into the lamplight. Nevertheless I felt as though their eyes were fixed on me and each man had a weapon in his pocket; but no one moved toward my end of the car.

There was no suspicion of the events that were going forward a few feet beyond the door and I doubt, even if it had been known, whether any one would have taken the chance of coming out of the door.

I must have been a formidable, mysterious figure. Although the youngest, I was the largest of the three men, and with the pistol in my hand and the "spook cap," as Mooney called it, it would have taken courage to have advanced against me.

It was the plan that when Mooney had finished with his work and had the loot in the sack ready to go he would pull the emergency air brake. This would stop the train instantly and we should all get off on the fireman's side of the train. He had explained to us in his lecture behind the water tank that train officials always look on the engineer's side when any trouble arises.

I do not know how it happened, but for some reason Mooney directed White to make this signal and by mistake he pulled the wrong cord.

That warned the engineer.

I felt the automatic air begin to clamp the brake shoes. The engineer blew four long sharp blasts to call the conductor forward. The conductor with the flagman at his heels started on the run. They had been sitting in the car before me, all the time under my eyes. Now they plunged through the door on to the platform.

I shouted at them as they advanced.

"Go back or I'll shoot you to death."

In my excitement I roared the words. They stopped suddenly like men who had come up against an invisible wall, dropped back through the door and closed it with a bang.

I heard Mooney call to me as he jumped down. I jumped with him.

By this time the train had stopped. The engineer was still blowing. The conductor had run to the rear of the train, it seems, when I had driven him back, and got a rifle, and was on the ground when I got off. He was shooting at Mooney and White as they disappeared through the bushes. He was almost up to me as I stood there on the step uncertain what to do. Then I remembered the direction Mooney had given, elevated the muzzle of the automatic and fired it in his face.

I did not hit him, but I got the result Mooney predicted.

He dropped the gun and fell back with a startled cry. I took the chance and plunged into the bushes after my companions. But my assault on his mind did not permanently disable him; he stooped over, groped for the rifle, got it in his hands, and began firing at me as I ran. Once he hit a tree so close to me that the splinters flew in my face, but in a moment I was covered by the wood.

I ran on for some distance and then squatted down behind a tree. But no one followed. For some time there were confused noises, voices scarcely audible at the distance; then the train moved on.

It was Mooney's direction that after the train had passed we should return to the water tank. "It would be better to go back at once," he said. There would be no posse for the train to leave, but later the authorities would be informed and search would be made for us.

I followed his direction.

But I must have gone farther than the others, for both he and White were behind the tank when I came up. He had lighted a little fire of twigs and leaves and in this we burned the "spook caps." I did not see the "loot sack" and I asked him about the Mexican money.

"No luck, my son," he said. "White had the wrong tip, but I am not a man to disappoint a lad. Here's twenty dollars for you. Meet the circus at Marysville."

He pointed out the direction through the fields.

I gave him back the automatic pistol and the railroad clothes and prepared to set out on my journey. It was not above half a dozen miles, he said, and I could not miss the way. He would show me. He climbed up on the crossbars of the water tank and pointed out the direction, the distant hilltop where I would find a turn of the road.

I was about to set out when he stopped me.

"Wait a moment," he said, "and I will put you clear of the bloodhounds."

He stooped and in the darkness carefully passed his hand over the soles of my shoes.

I went up the railroad track until I was clear of the wood, climbed the hill, and got down into the road. I had become an outlaw, a member of the most daring gang of train robbers in all the annals of that high-handed crime.

CHAPTER II

THE HOLDUP

I slept that morning in the hay beyond the horse stalls.

It was afternoon before I wakened. I had gotten into the town just as the circus was unloading, and, as it happened, the road upon which I approached came first to the switch on which the horse cars were standing.

The one thing about which I had any knowledge, in the whole circus, was horses.

I stopped at the car and helped the man get the horses out. It was doubtless a fortunate coincidence, because I fell in as a sort of assistant to the man who had charge of the horse car, and it gave me a kind of connection with the circus. I helped him get the animals over to the field and under the horse tent, and when they had been cared for I went to sleep.

I had now some money in my pocket and I sauntered about on that afternoon, pleased with everything.

The experience of robbing my first train did not seem to affect me. It was a sort of adventure whose elements of danger I had escaped, and it was now ended. I seemed not to realize that there was any further peril about it.

I saw Mooney in the afternoon in his canvas chair. He paid no attention to me. White I saw a little later. It was at the evening performance. I was helping to take away the horses that appeared in the ring. I was not in the main circus tent but in an attached tent in which the performers mounted.

I was bringing out a horse for one of these riders when White came up.

There were two persons standing near the horse: a young girl dressed like a fairy—dainty and lovely, I thought, in her gauze skirts and gilded butterfly wings—and a little woman. This woman was small and dark haired with narrow eyes and flat ears set close to her head. She turned viciously on White when he came up.

"Don't go near her!" she cried. "Don't even look at her!"

"You are a fool, Maggie," he said. "I want to speak to the boy."

She turned suddenly toward me as though she had not noticed me before.

"Where did you come from?" she said. Then she laughed. "It don't matter. I know where you are going."

And she went out toward the entrance to the circus tent, following the big white horse that carried the fairy.

White said only a few words to me when she was gone.

"Hang along with the circus; we have got straight dope on that Mexican money and we'll pick it up in a few days."

I traveled with the circus as one might travel with a fairy caravan. Everything was of the deepest and newest interest.

But the greatest wonder was the girl who rode the white horse. The little, determined, black-haired woman was always with her. I saw her only when I helped her into the saddle and took away the horse.

She stood between the girl and everybody.

There was no exception, but she did not seem to consider me. Once or twice I saw her looking curiously at me when I brought the horse to help the girl into the saddle.

Sometimes she talked with Mooney.

I suppose a week passed in this fashion; then one evening, as I was helping to bed down the horses, White came into the tent. The evening performance had ended and it was perhaps midnight.

"We are going to take a little motor ride," he said. "Come along."

I went with him.

We made a detour of the circus field and came into the border of the town. It was a residence street of the better class of houses. It was late and the lights of the street had been put out. We stopped finally before a garage in a lot between two houses. The door to the garage was locked and White turned the lock with some implement which I could not see.

Then we went inside and carefully pushed the car out into the street.

White locked the door again behind us. We pushed the car along the street for perhaps a hundred yards before we got in. The man understood the motor perfectly and we slipped along the street and out of the town.

At a bridge on the outskirts we picked up Mooney. He had his bundle as on our first adventure.

White ran the car at great speed for perhaps two hours; then we pulled up by the roadside and stopped.

Before we got out of the car I had an explanation of Mooney's occult device against the bloodhound.

There was a mist of fog. It had begun to gather over the lowland. We had noticed it—a white blanket lying on the fields as we came along. It was now rising, but it came up slowly as though it were a sort of impalpable stratum formed mysteriously out of the earth and extending, under some mathematical direction, upward. It was like a piece of enchantment in the manner in which the thing arose. It now lay on the world about us extending to the macadam road.

Mooney took a flash light out of his pocket.

It was not the usual cylinder affair. It was, rather, a little squat lantern with a bull's-eye bulb; thick—necessarily so, I imagine—for there was a powerful light concentrated on the small disc and it, therefore, required a considerable battery.

He looked at the clock on the motor.

"We shall have some time to wait," he said, "but the fog may increase and we ought to look over the ground."

I got up to get out of the car, when he put his hand on my arm.

"My son," he said, "the bloodhound will be no friend of ours; let us think of him before he thinks of us."

He went on in a drawling voice.

"Every little sheriff," he said, "has fitted himself out with one of these trailing beasts."

Then he laughed.

"They will be valuable, no doubt, for Little Eva and the ice, but for us they will hardly constitute a menace."

He reached into his pocket and took out a flask of what one might imagine to be brandy.

"I have here," he said, "a lotion to confuse his nose."

He drew out the stopper, poured the liquid into his hand, and rubbed it carefully over our shoes. I knew on the instant, by the odor, it was turpentine. Mooney was very careful about this thing. The whole of our shoes were carefully painted with the turpentine. He explained the theory of the thing while he was at work.

"It makes me laugh," he said, "to think how our brethren of the road have been chased about by dogs.... It is ridiculous to be chased by anything, especially a creature depending on its nose. It is the fine discriminating sense of odors that distinguishes the bloodhound. If our footweary predecessors had only thought about it they might have saved themselves the walking.

"How does one destroy a delicate odor?

"The solution is simple—by laying down over it a heavier, gross one. And here one must consider the instinct of the bloodhound. He will follow the trail of a man, that is, something living, a thing which he has observed to move, but he will not follow the trail of a pine tree. Turpentine, to the dog's sensitive nose, is a tremendous stench that he will walk away from."

The road, as I have said, ran parallel to the track. We got out now and went directly across the field to the railroad. Here, close beside the track, Mooney set up a piece of rotten cross tie. It was to be a signal, as I later discovered; and we should return this way.

Then he walked back along the track. I was perhaps at something more than half a mile that we came to a semaphore. It was only in the knowledge of future events that I understood what we were about to do; and it is in the light of this knowledge that I am able to describe what happened.

The men had determined to hold up the through passenger train from Washington to New Orleans. Their original intention was to stop this train at a water tank but for some reason they gave up this plan; I think it was because knowledge of the other train robbery made them fear that the usual stopping places would be watched. So they determined upon another device. A macadamized road paralleled the railroad track and they decided to commandeer a motor car, follow the track to some isolated point, and there stop the train.

This road had what is known as the block system of signals; that is to say, every mile along the track there was a semaphore which informed the engineer whether or not there was another train in the same block or on the same track.

In the day this signaling is done by painted arms and at night by red, green, and white lights: the red light meaning to come to a full stop until the white light is shown; the green light meaning that the train is in the block and half through it; and the white light meaning that the train is through the block and is at least a mile distant.

It was Mooney's plan to short circuit two of the wires of the semaphore and make such connection that the red light would show.

When we were on the ground before the track, White, who seemed the mechanic, tried to accomplish this. But the semaphore arm kept turning around and around and would not stop.

It was the ingenious Mooney who found a way out of this difficulty.

"Take off the short-circuit wire," he said; "climb the semaphore pole and tie the red arm down so it will show all the time."

When White found out that the semaphore could be thus managed he left it as it was, restoring its proper connections.

Mooney had practically the same outfit we had used on the previous occasion, except that he had invented a new kind of mask. This mask was made so that it was placed in the hat and could not be seen. It had a hem at the bottom, entirely around, and filled with shot so that, immediately on lifting the hat, the mask dropped over the face and stayed there.

There were no holes in it except two round ones for eyes.

We got into our disguises and waited for the train.

In order to make no mistake, it was the plan of this man to sit fast until we heard the through train blow for a station, two miles away. That would give us time to fix the semaphore.

It seemed a long time as we sat there in the darkness waiting for the train; but it was perhaps, in fact, less than half an hour. Directly we heard the whistle in the distance and we went down to the track; White had got a piece of fence wire and he now climbed the pole and tied the red semaphore arm down over the green and white lights. Mooney went about fifty yards along the track in the direction from which the train was coming, and waited at the place where he thought the engine would stop. White and I hid ourselves where he thought the baggage and express cars would stop.

But our calculations were not accurate.

Instead of the engine stopping where we thought it would, it ran on for at least a hundred yards past the red light. There was a fog, and the engineer did not see the red signal soon enough. The train roared past us. We knew the engineer had thrown on the emergency, "goosed the air" as White called it. The fire from the brake shoes grinding on the wheels showed up red along the whole train. The engineer reversed and brought back his engine to the point where Mooney was hidden behind a tree on the right of way. The engineer was following a rule of the road that one must not under any circumstances run past a red light.

We jumped at once.

Mooney climbed into the engine and took charge of the fireman and engineer. They made no resistance to the masked man with a weapon in his hand. White rushed in and uncoupled the mail and express cars from the rest of the train.

Now, on these through first-class passenger trains, a power velocipede, or what is known in the dialect of the road as a "gasoline speeder," is always carried in the baggage car. It is an emergency vehicle in order to enable one of the crew to get to a telegraph station in case of a wreck or any accident. When the engine stopped under this unexpected red light of the semaphore a negro porter, seeing two masked men, ran to the baggage car and got the vehicle out on the ground. He was lifting it on his shoulder.

I did not understand what the thing meant at the time, but I called to White and he came out from behind the two cars.

The porter found himself before the round end of an automatic.

"Put that thing back," said White, "or I'll blow your head off."

The man turned with the vehicle in his hands, thrust it back into the baggage car and dropped where he stood, his face down, by the side of the track.

By this time the passengers began to come off to see what had happened to the train.

I don't know precisely what I did, but to White there was no confusion. He ordered every one back into the train and began to fire along the sides to hurry them into the covering of the cars. In the meantime, Mooney had brought the engineer and fireman back to the mail car and had taken the mail clerks out of the car.

There had been no resistance to this man.

He shot out one or two of the windows to add emphasis to his directions, but it was an emphasis that had not been needed. No thought of resistance had occurred to anybody. Mooney sent the trainmen to the rear. He impressed upon them that any man appearing outside of the train would be killed.

In the whirl of these events I seemed to be little more than a spectator.

To the train crew I was the third menacing figure, masked and armed, but I am not certain what benefit I would have been to the two men in a sudden emergency. It was my direction to stay with White and I now ran with him to the engine. Mooney took charge of the end of the train where White had cut it off. He stood on the platform of the mail car.

We climbed up into the engine, White and I, and at once I saw that this man knew precisely what to do. He threw the air brake into release, dropped his reversing lever forward, opened the throttle and started out like a skilled engineer.

He put me to shoveling coal into the engine.

"Make a green fire," he said. "We shall stop shortly, and if we need to start again we shall have a heavy fire ready."

I did not know at the time what he meant by a green fire, but I knew that he wished coal shoveled into the engine; I followed that direction. We pulled down the track perhaps a half mile until we reached the piece of rotten cross tie that Mooney had set up. Then we stopped.

In every detail White handled the engine with skill.

Long afterward I realized fully what he was about. Before we got down he put on the injector and filled the boiler with water up to the third gauge so there would be no danger of its running dry and burning out the crown sheet. He wished that train to go on and he did not propose to disable it.

When we were on the ground he gave me definite orders.

I was to stand beside the engine and if anybody appeared in any direction of the track I was to fire the automatic. He even stopped to show me how the weapon worked, slipping back the top of it with his hand so that, cocked and released, I had only to pull the trigger with my finger.

Then he went down the side of the train to the express car.

I did not know until afterward the trouble in that car.

The men could find nothing of value. They ripped open the sealed express, but they got little. As it afterward developed there was, in fact, forty thousand dollars in currency in the car. But the express messenger had taken a precaution against a holdup.

He had wrapped the packages of currency in old newspapers and laid them on the floor of the car.

When it came out in the newspaper reports of the holdup White cursed viciously; he had kicked these packages out of the way, with his foot, when he and Mooney had searched the car.

The two men were gone a long time; disappointed in the express, they had searched the registered mail.

As I stood there on the track before the engine I had a strange sensation. It was very still; there was a ghostly fog, and somewhere beyond me, as though out of the sky, I heard whispering voices.

I strained my ears to listen, standing as one does on tiptoe.

But I could not be certain. No word was audible to me nor any decided voice, but now and then there seemed to be a murmuring in the fog, and, what was beyond understanding, it seemed behind the engine in the clouded sky.

What human creatures could thus whisper in the sky?

Mooney and White returned presently in no very pleasant mood. I think the time taken with the thing made them uneasy. White had the loot sack and we started along across the field, to where we had left the automobile on the road.

It was then that I got the explanation of the mysterious voices.

There were three hobos riding on the top of the mail car. They had been witnesses of everything that had occurred. They sat there like immense buzzards outlined against the dim light of the sky. Mooney stopped a moment. He seemed to reflect, turning his weapon about in his hand. Then he spoke to the derelicts on the top of the car.

"If they pinch you for this job," he said, "write me a letter."

And he went on.

I thought for a moment that he intended to shoot the men, but no such idea was passing through his mind. It had occurred to him that, perhaps, these unfortunate derelicts would be charged with the robbery.

And, as it happened, they were in very grave danger.

The posse that gathered, seeing them on the top of the car, opened a fusillade. It was very lucky that the idea occurred to Mooney, for, as it happened, these men drew all the suspicion of the officials. Three men had held up the train. They were three men. They were afterwards tried before the District Court of the United States and very nearly convicted. No doubt they often recalled those significant words of Mooney's. But unfortunately he had left them no address to which their communication could be sent.

When we got to the car Mooney again turned his lantern on the clock. He swore softly; then he stood back a moment in reflection.

"We're late," he said, "I don't see how we could have taken up so much time on this job; it was the cursed mail."

White did not speak and I remained silent, standing by the little man now motionless in reflection.

I suppose it must have been five minutes ticked off by the clock while he stood there. Then suddenly he came to a conclusion.

"Give me the spook faces," he said.

He meant the masks under the hats. I handed him my hat, pulling the mask up over my face. He seized White's, drew off his own, and disappeared in the direction of the track from which we had just come.

I did not understand what the man was about, and I think White was equally in the dark. But it was clear that the unexpected lateness of the hour had put some of his calculations out of joint. White got into the car and sat down at the wheel. The loot sack was already in the tonneau and I got in beside it.

The fog had now come up thinly above the road.

It seemed to me that we had scarcely occupied the time it required to get into the car when Mooney returned. He seemed to appear as an apparition out of the mist. He got at once into the car and spoke to White.

"Here's the engineer's cap," he said. "I got it out of the box under the seat in the engine." He put it on.

"Now swing her round and step on her."

He meant for White to turn the car and go back at the greatest speed he could. The man, as I have said, was an expert with a motor. He was only a moment at the turn and we were presently racing along the road.

I did not understand what Mooney meant.

We all wore the blue jackets and overalls in which we had held up the train. It was the distinguishing uniform of the train crew, and now with Mooney wearing the engineer's cap it seemed to me that we had simply marked ourselves for certain identification.

But it was the reflection of inexperience.

Mooney, when he looked at the clock, foresaw what we were certain to meet on the road and he skillfully prepared for it. Two miles down the road was the station.

We raced toward it.

Suddenly, it seemed to me, a light loomed in the road, and another, and in a moment we had come into a crowd of motor cars, trucks, and the like, packed with men. It was the posse that Mooney knew would come out from the town in the unexpected lapse of time. He foresaw that the train crew would get the information of the holdup to the town and it was this posse that we must be prepared to meet. If we had got away earlier we could have passed the town before the posse had assembled, but having taken so much time it was certain to be on the way.

Had I been in control of the party, or White or any man of lesser resources than this clever bandit, the search for the train robbers would have ended there in the road.

But this person, called Mooney, was an extraordinary human creature.

It was not the bloodhound alone that he was able to outwit. When he found the posse must be met, he prepared to meet it in the only way certain of success.

He leaned over and whispered some direction to White when the lights appeared, and we pulled up into the very crowd of motors.

My heart seemed to rise and fill my throat.

I saw, in a sort of confusion, the vehicles in the road; a motor just a little ahead of us with some men; a truck before us driven by a negro; a man in a hunting coat with a shotgun and two dogs—the bloodhounds for which we had prepared; a low roadster almost beside us.

It was the posse keeping together.

They had seen our lights and were prepared to stop us. The men stood up with their weapons in their hands, an array of indiscriminate firearms. Our motor did not entirely stop. We slowed down, running into the crowd of men. Mooney got on his feet, shouting:

"We have 'em surrounded in the express car. Get there as fast as you can; we've got to go into the town for gasoline.... Don't stand here. Hurry!"

To the posse the explanation was complete.

We were a party of the train crew; one could clearly see that. What Mooney said coincided with the report that had come in to them.

We did not wait for these men to reflect about it. We ran on past, Mooney shouting to them to make haste; that there was a man in the road with a lantern to stop them.

"Let your cars out," he cried, "for God's sake."

And we went on.

It was the only adventure on the way. The road skirted the town, and once past it Mooney considered the peril ended. We took off the trainmen's uniforms and put them into the sack.

The fog increased, it seemed to me, but its very density covered the close of our adventure. We ran along the street to the garage from which we had borrowed the car. White handled it with skill. He entered the street with a spurt of speed, then he cut off the engine and we glided almost noiselessly along to the very door of the garage. We got down. White unlocked the door and we pushed the car in; then he locked it again carefully.

I don't think he had a key; I think he manipulated that lock with a bent nail. But at any rate we walked away, having restored the car to its house,

Mooney with the loot sack on his shoulder. It was Saturday night and the circus remained over until Sunday in the meadow beyond the town.

Only the top of the great tent stood now above the sheet of fog as we set out across the field toward it.

CHAPTER III

THE BLOODHOUNDS

I think the third holdup undertaken by these men was the most remarkable that ever occurred in all the history of train robberies.

I do not mean that the result of it was so remarkable or that it was attended by peculiar adventures. But the cool nerve exhibited by Mooney—his deliberate assumption of enormous risk, and his plan to draw the attention of the authorities from his confederate—marks the affair as without equal. The plan, too, to get away with what was taken in the robbery was wholly original. In all record of criminal methods I have never known this plan to be adopted by anybody else.

I think it was worked out by Mooney to meet a situation which he knew now existed.

The two train robberies which we had undertaken had aroused the country. The authorities could be expected to make every effort to run down and capture the highwayman who should undertake a repetition of these affairs. Mooney knew this and he worked out a plan to meet it.

The circus was loaded and moving when I first learned of this new adventure.

I was sitting in the box car with the horses. We had pulled up on a siding near some little town. The door was open and Mooney and White came in. White was very carefully dressed. He wore a new overcoat and derby hat and he carried a leather suit case. He looked precisely like one of the thousand traveling men who go about over the country. When the two men got into the car, I did not know who was with White, Mooney was so changed.

I looked at him with astonishment. I could not believe that the person before me was the man with whom I had been so closely associated. He had a heavy drooping mustache, long black hair and deep-lined face. His eyes seemed lengthened and narrowed, and he appeared taller and more erect.

Now, the man naturally in life was stooped, and with a weary, nervous appearance, as though every motion were an effort. This attitude, as I have come to know, was the languor of a drug and his common appearance was the result of the use of it.

But to-day, by some powerful effort, or perhaps by virtue of an excessive injection of the drug itself, his whole manner had changed. Of course the appearance of the man was merely the result of the make-up, amazingly skillful, which he had undertaken for the thing he had in hand.

He explained to me that they had finally located the treasure train and that they were going to hold it up to-night. He said that we would probably be noticed and that it was necessary to change our appearance so descriptions of us, which would be published abroad over the country, would be wholly misleading.

I had been sleeping on some blankets in the horse car. There was only a box for a chair. He directed me to sit down on the box; fastened a horse blanket under my coat, between the shoulders, to make a hump; and then he began to transform me into somebody else. The man worked very carefully on my face and hair for perhaps an hour, in the horse car. It was nearly dark. The train had gone on and the door was closed. Mooney worked by the light of a lantern which I carried in the horse car. Finally, when he had finished, he held up a little hand mirror so that I might see the result of his work.

I was astonished at the face I saw.

In that hour, under Mooney's skillful manipulation, I had become middle aged. My hair was streaked with gray; my face was lined. The thing was like a piece of sorcery. There was a delicate network of wrinkles about the eyes; there was even the sagging of age beginning to appear in the outline of jaw and throat.

The man's skill was uncanny.

He had transformed himself into a straight, vigorous motion-picture desperado of middle life, turning the evidences of age backward in his own case, while he carried them forward in mine. No one could have known us for the same men; the transformation was too complete. We were, in fact, not the same men; there could be no possibility of those who would recognize us now ever being able to identify us when these disguises were removed.

Mooney had with him a second of these leather suit cases, precisely in every detail like the large one which White carried. He told me nothing except that I was to go with him.

It was late of a Sunday evening. The circus train was making a long run. About dark, as the train was going slowly, White got out. I afterward learned that it was his plan to take a street car from this point to a station where we were to board a through express.

About nine o'clock the train pulled into a town.

When it began to slow up, Mooney and I got out and closed the door. We followed a road into town. Turning into the main street, we walked leisurely over to the railroad station. Mooney, walking with a brisk, active step, carried the leather suit case, and I trudged beside him.

The town was evidently not very large and the through express made only a short stop.

There was a line of people waiting to get on the train, standing outside the station on the wooden platform. We went down through this crowd to one end of it, for it was Mooney's intention to take the day coach nearest to the express car. Here I saw White waiting with his suit case, as though he were an ordinary traveler.

When the train pulled in we got on with the other passengers.

We sat down about midway of the coach, but I noticed that White, who was among the first to get on the train, went forward to the very end of the coach and sat down on the last seat. At the next station Mooney and I got off; we walked to the head end of the train and when it started we climbed up the steps of this forward coach next to the express car, as though we were going into the car from the forward end of it. But we did not go in. We stopped on the steps while the train pulled out.

I suppose we remained there for perhaps twenty minutes, until the lights of the town disappeared and the train trailed out into the great open country.

Then Mooney proceeded to put his plan for the holdup into operation.

He went over to the door of the express car and knocked on it. One of the biggest men I have ever seen opened the door. Mooney's weapon seemed to appear suddenly almost in the man's face. He stepped back with a little cry, and we were instantly in the express car with the door closed and locked behind us. There were two other men in this car, and on top of the safe were a rifle and a short automatic shotgun. The men for whom these weapons were provided made no effort to avail themselves of them. They stood in the middle of the car with their hands up as far as they could reach, their eyes wide, their mouths gaping.

I think our appearance struck them with more terror than if we had been masked highwaymen. Mooney was so evidently the stage type of Western desperado; and I must have been, myself, a sinister figure—a strange figure, with the big leather suit case in one hand and an automatic pistol in the other. Mooney ordered the two men at the end of the car to lie down on their faces; this they did with ludicrous haste; one of them nearly fell in his effort to obey the order quickly. They went even further than Mooney directed; they lay flat with their arms around their faces as though to convince the outlaw that they would make no efforts to see what was going on.

Mooney ordered the big man to open the safe.

The man was evidently in terror, but he was a sensible person. He pointed out that he could not open it; that it had a time lock on it. He went ahead of Mooney to the safe, squatted down in the car and put his big finger on the lock.

"You can see," he said, "I can't open it."

The man's face was distended with anxiety.

What he said was the truth, but he was not certain that the highwayman, standing a few feet behind him covering him with a weapon, would believe what he said. He knew the stories of such holdups: how express messengers had been ordered to open safes and when they refused, or where unable to do so, they had been promptly shot.

I think the man expected to be shot, as he squatted there beside the safe, his big body loose, his face covered with sweat. Mooney saw instantly that the man was telling the truth. I do not know that he was, in fact, paying any attention to what the man said. He knew at a glance that the safe was fitted with a time lock.

He advanced toward the man, and the express messenger's face seemed to puff out as though it were becoming suddenly swollen; I think he was now convinced that the highwayman was about to kill him. But instead, Mooney ordered him to lie down. He turned over on the floor precisely like one who collapses from fatigue.

Mooney took the leather suit case from my hand.

"Shoot any man that moves," he said hoarsely.

Then he went to work at the safe. The big messenger was so close to the safe door that Mooney had literally to push his body out of the way with his foot. Mooney got some tools out of the dress-suit case, drilled the combination, and put in a charge of nitroglycerine.

He did it quickly, with incredible skill.

Then he ordered the express messenger to move up to the end of the car.

"Go ahead," he said, "or you will be shot full of scrap iron."

The big man got up on his hands and knees and without turning his head crawled to the end of the car and lay down.

Mooney took the horse blanket from under my coat, and whatever else he could find in the car, and heaped them against the door of the safe. Then he fired the nitroglycerine. He had gauged the explosion to do exactly what he wished it to do. There was a dull sound and a jar, but far less noise than I expected. The blanket and coats that Mooney had heaped up against the safe were hardly thrown down, but the combination was broken open and the man was able to manipulate the tumblers.

In a very few minutes he succeeded in opening the safe.

There was another small steel door fastened with a lock. Mooney did not even take time to get the key for this door from the express messenger. He took a bunch of keys out of his own pocket, selected a flat one, and turned the lock. He did it instantly, as though a lock of this sort could be opened by a twist of the fingers.

There were a number of big brown envelopes sealed with red wax. These Mooney packed in the dress-suit case; then he got up and we went back to the door of the car through which we had entered. Mooney opened the door and motioned me to step through it out on the platform; then he spoke as though I still remained in the car.

"Keep these men covered," he said, in the same harsh voice, "and if one of them moves shoot him. I am going through the passenger coaches."

He stepped through the door and slammed it behind him. We were both now on the outside of the express car. But in the imagination of the men lying on the floor within it, one of the desperate highwaymen remained, covering them with his weapon.

Mooney went ahead of me to the passenger car. He had the leather dress-suit case in one hand and his automatic pistol in the other. I followed behind him. He opened the door, and, entering the car, he stood a moment looking at the amazed passengers. There was hardly a sound, but astonishment brought everybody in the car even those half asleep, up straining in their seats.

The highwayman of the storybooks was before them.

Mooney remained thus motionless for a moment until everybody in the car could get the picture in his mind, then he spoke quick and sharp.

"Turn," he said, "—everybody—and face the other way."

The passengers turned instantly; no man hesitated. The direction was obeyed as though it were an order of a drill sergeant. White, who sat at the end of the car, turned with the others.

Mooney stood in the aisle just beside this last seat in which White had been sitting. He now put down his suit case and reached up, pulled the emergency cord, and stopped the train. Then he picked up the suit case and stepped back through the door to where I stood on the platform.

Here a puzzling thing happened.

Mooney did not pick up the same suit case he put down; but he slid the case into the seat where White was sitting and took up the case White had beside him. They were precisely alike, and no one but myself saw the exchange made. The passengers were facing the other way.

When the train slowed up we jumped down. Mooney gave me the suit case to carry. There was nothing in it, as I afterward discovered, but a couple of bricks.

It was pitch dark. We both started straight off from the train. I was ahead of Mooney.

I suppose I was about a hundred feet from the track when I went down suddenly into a ditch; the dirt was soft and I was not hurt. I must have fallen at least six feet. The train was still standing; the people in the coaches had gotten out. We could hear them talking and we could, of course, see the lights of the train. Mooney must have seen me fall, for he slipped down into the ditch and spoke to me softly. There might be a guard of some sort on the train and it was advisable for us to keep in the ditch instead of climbing out on the farther side.

We moved along the ditch as quickly as we could, for, I suppose, a distance of some three hundred feet. Here we found a railroad tie which some one had put across for a foot bridge. Mooney reached up and caught the tie with his hands and climbed out; I followed his example, passing up the suit case for him to hold until I got out. We stood still for a moment, listening; presently we heard the train pull out.

Mooney then led the way back to the railroad track. He seemed to wish to get his bearings of the country. He seemed to know where he was, although as I have said the night was dark, and we started down the track in the direction from which the train had come. We followed the track for about a mile until we came to a deep rock cut. This cut seemed to be the indicatory point for which Mooney was looking, and he at once began to run.

I followed him.

The cut seemed endless, and in spite of our speed I could see the outlines rise higher and higher against the sky until the walls seemed perpendicular, as though the track was cut down through solid rock. The cut must have been over a mile long, for I was nearly worn out when we reached the end of it.

Then we turned off sharply to the right. The country seemed open and I followed Mooney, who walked swiftly across fields, until finally we got into a road. I had no idea where we were going, or the direction, except that it seemed to be at right angles to the railway and through a country that Mooney knew. Taking the rock cut for a point of departure, he was endeavoring to find this road which we finally came into.

When we reached the road Mooney took the suit case, opened it, threw away the bricks, carried it on for perhaps a mile, and tossed it into a fence corner. I now understood what the man was doing. He was making a deliberate trail for any one who should follow; this would enable White to escape easily with the suit case which contained what had been taken out of the express safe.

The posse which would presently come to the scene of the robbery with the inevitable bloodhound would have no difficulty in following our trail. Any number of persons on the train could identify us and would remember that we carried the dress-suit case. The expressman would identify it as being the one he had seen in Mooney's hand and into which we had packed the contents of the safe.

We continued to travel the road, running, as I afterward discovered, due east, and about daylight we came to another railroad line. When we reached this track Mooney stopped.

He explained then what he had been about.

It was his intention that there should be a plain trail which the posse could follow across the country. The trail should end here, so it would be evident that the robbers had boarded some train passing on this track, perhaps a freight. The energies of the authorities would then be directed toward the search of this railroad. They would endeavor to find what trains passed in the night, and their destination, and the whole search would be turned in this direction.

He now turpentined our shoes very carefully, and our clothing.

It was beginning to be daylight, and I could see something of the lie of the country. We had come through a valley, but off to our right there was the loom of a mountain. We went down the track for perhaps half a mile; then we turned up into a wood and began the ascent of the mountain.

The sun was up and we finally stopped in a wooded thicket on a sort of knoll that overlooked the country. The valley we had crossed stretched away to the west. The mountain seemed also to lie in that direction. The railroad track extended at the foot of the mountain below us, and from the point where we were hidden in the thicket, on the little shoulder or knoll, I could see clearly the way over which we had come and the point where we had emerged on the track.

Mooney had some food: dried meat and hard biscuit. We ate our breakfast, and he went to sleep, curling up in the leaves of the thicket as though nothing extraordinary had happened, and he was peacefully in a bed.

I could not go to sleep.

The incidents of the adventure in which I had become involved ran vaguely through my mind.

I am now certain that the explanation these men gave of their failure to find anything of value in the two preceding holdups was false; but it was clear that they were disappointed. They were on the lookout for some large shipment of money which they expected to obtain. I do not know whether they had any definite information about such a probable shipment or whether they were merely trying chances for it.

The story of the Mexican government money was, of course, merely a pretense.

Looking at the thing now, it seems to me that I was not very much impressed with that feature of the affair. It was a series of adventures directed against my enemy, the railroad, somewhat as the fairy adventures of the storybooks were directed against a dragon.

Mooney had given me a hundred dollars, not as part of the loot—for they continued to insist that they had not found what they were looking for—but as an honorarium out of his own pocket.

This was a large sum of money to me.

I do not remember precisely to what use I put the money except in one shining instance. I bought a bracelet for the girl who rode the white horse in the circus. It was a gold chain fastened with a lock.

And it very nearly caused a tragedy.

The little dark-haired woman Maggie, who was with the girl always, like her shadow, noticed it immediately. I had given it to the girl when she went into the afternoon performances. When she came out Maggie seized her wrist, indicating the bracelet with some query. The girl pointed toward me where, at some distance, I stood by White near the horse tent. The little woman thought she meant White, and she rushed at him like a mad dog. From somewhere about her, as though out of the air, a knife flashed in her hand.

The thing happened in a moment.

White caught her by the shoulder and threw his body backward, but she swung under his arm and struck at him. Fortunately her reach was not quite long enough and the knife only slashed his coat. I caught the woman's arm. But it was all the two of us could manage to hold her. She cursed and struggled like a harpy.

Mooney came sauntering up.

"It wasn't White, Maggie," he drawled; "it was the boy."

The woman instantly ceased to struggle. We released her and she stood for a moment looking at me, as though in some deep reflection. Then she spoke.

"Why did you give it to her?"

I was embarrassed to reply. Finally I stammered it out.

"I don't know.... I like her."

She remained looking at me, her eyes narrowed, her hand extended across the lower part of her face. But she did not go any farther with her inquiry. Mooney continued in his relaxed drawl.

"What's the notion, Maggie?" he said. "The girl's not your child."

She swung slowly toward him.

"Not your cursed notion!" she said, indicating me with a gesture. And then she walked away.

I thought the thing out and in my youthful fancy the girl became the fairy princess for which she each day made up. This woman was not her mother. She was some royal foundling, changed by the fairies or stolen at her birth. I treasured every word with her, every touch of her hand, every look she gave me.

I thought about it as I sat there hidden by the undergrowth.

Then, suddenly, something caught my eye.

Far out in the valley in the direction from which we had come I noticed a sort of blur; presently it became a group of dots moving about, as one has observed minute organisms under a microscope. The tiny things advanced until I presently saw that it was a crowd of men; then in the distance I heard the baying of the dogs.

They seemed to come slowly.

The sound of the dogs increased and in a little while I could make out individuals of the posse. A tall man moved in front holding two dogs on the leash. They came along our trail right down to the railroad. There the dogs stopped and I realized the efficacy of Mooney's precaution against the bloodhound. When the dogs reached the place where we had turpentined our shoes, they stopped instantly and began to howl.

The man led them about in circles, across the track and beyond it, in every direction, but the dogs would not take up our trail. The turpentine was a complete safeguard against them; they would not follow it. The big man handled the dogs with skill; he moved out in an ever widening circle; he covered the ground for a hundred yards in every direction, from the point where our trail stopped, but it was no use.

The dogs would not take up a trail fouled with turpentine.

The posse then gathered in a sort of council, and I sat watching them through the thicket. They evidently came to the one obvious solution of the matter—that the train robbers whom they had followed to the track had, here, boarded some passing train; and they set out southward along the track to what I imagine was the closest railway station.

This was precisely the thing Mooney intended them to do.

He was so certain that they would do it that he slept peacefully while this posse was within a quarter of a mile of us, and the dogs baying along the edge of the mountain in which we were at that moment concealed. I felt a vast relief when the posse departed, and I lay back on the dry leaves with my hands linked under my head.

I must have fallen asleep, for when I awoke it was midday. Mooney had found a little stream and had removed all the evidences of his disguise. The wig he had buried under a stone and the make-up he had removed from his face.

He took me through the bushes to the little rivulet, a mere thread of water from some spring, and very carefully restored me to my normal appearance. He removed the make-up with some sort of grease and I washed my hair in the water which he had dammed up into a tiny pool.

We now bore no relation, in our outward appearance, to the men who had held up the train.

It was afternoon and we set out west through the edge of the mountain. The going was rough and dangerous. We found deep gullies and ravines that ran almost from the top of the mountain into the very valleys. Some of these walls were almost perpendicular. They looked to stand sheer for a hundred feet.

We had to follow these gullies for a great distance up the mountain before we could cross them. Then, we came to ledges of rock which it was impossible for us to scale; these we had to follow down the mountain.

I suggested to Mooney that it would be easier to take a road, but he replied that the news of the holdup would be generally over the country and that it would be dangerous for strangers to be found on any of the roads. He said the plan was to follow the mountain until we came to the river about twenty miles farther west, and then to go down the river to a town from which we could take a train.

As night came on we descended to the border of the mountain and followed it west. About daylight we reached the river. We traveled two or three miles over muddy ground and through weeds and grasses to our waists, following down the river, looking for some chance boat. Finally by a fallen tree we found a skiff. This boat had been anchored in low water and the river afterward had risen and covered it. It was now half full of mud.

We had to clean it out; there were no oars but Mooney got a piece of board from a fence and we shoved off the boat and started down the river. It was a heavenly sensation after the immense labor of that night's travel through the mountain. Mooney was trying to locate the town at which he intended to stop and take a passenger train. He thought the town was nearer to the river than it actually was, but, as the river was low and the banks high, we failed to locate it until we had passed it for a mile.

And here we came very nearly into a tragedy.

It seemed that this river was the highway of bootleggers who were accustomed to bring liquor down into the state from a neighboring city. We did not know this. But we discovered, later, that every boat going down the river was searched. We were moving slowly between the high banks when we heard a motor boat and saw that we were being followed.

Mooney realized at once that it was of no use to endeavor to escape.

He told me to put my hand down into the water and drop the automatic pistol; he did the same, and before the boat was on us we were rid of any incriminating evidence. We did not know why we were being followed or why there was a motor boat on the river. It was barely possible that it was a party of the posse on the lookout for the men who had held up the train.

There was only one course open to us—to face them as though we were without concern.

Mooney stopped the skiff when the motor boat appeared and waited for it to come up. Some one—I think it was a constable—called to us when they approached.

"Hello, boys!" he said. "What have you got this morning?"

Mooney replied that he did not understand, and, without a further word, they pulled up where they could see into our boat. We did not know what they were about to do.

"We thought you might have a cargo of wet goods," the constable said.

Mooney did not reply and the man added:

"You boys live down the river, don't you?"

"Yes," said Mooney.

And with that the conversation ended and the motor boat went on.

We drifted down the river until we were out of sight of the motor boat. Then we returned along the road to the town which we had passed. Here we got our dinner at a restaurant, and calmly, like any other passengers, walked over to the station and a train.

CHAPTER IV

THE SECRET AGENT

Mooney's experience with the last holdup made him consider a plan more daring than any former adventure.

When the men came to examine the packages which Mooney had taken out of the safe on the through express and which White had so skillfully carried away through the trick of the exchanged suit case, they found that what they had taken to be money was, in fact, bonds of an industrial corporation, being shipped by sealed express.

This was a profound disappointment.

The bonds could not be negotiated, for they were registered. Mooney thought he might be able to obtain some reward, and I think he did take the matter up with a "fence" in one of the eastern cities.

The result of this ill fortune was that he determined on some plan by which he would be able, at his leisure, to examine the sealed express before taking it out of the car, for Mooney had always hated having to hurry away without sorting the loot. And, with this intention as a moving factor, he formulated a holdup so daring that it would never have occurred to a person of less determined assurance.

I have thought it advisable not to set out here the name of the town, as it would serve to identify persons who ought not to be held responsible for the fact that they were taken in by Mooney's ingenious plan.

We had resorted to no sort of disguise, except that both Mooney and White were very well dressed. White had with him a small telegraphic instrument in a paper box, and Mooney had one of those strapped leather bags that are sometimes carried by physicians. Mooney and I went on into the town, but White left the train some distance east of that point.

It was about six o'clock when Mooney and I arrived. We went directly from the railroad station to the sheriff's office, in the basement of the courthouse. Black letters painted on the window indicated it.

Mooney and I went down into the basement of the building, entered this office, and inquired for the sheriff. A girl was making out some tax receipts at a long wooden table. She said the sheriff was in the other room, got up, opened the door, and we entered.

The sheriff was a little red-haired man. He looked up as we came in, and turned over quickly a telegram which he had, apparently, just opened and which was lying on the table before him.

Mooney at once addressed him.

"My name is Jarvis," he said, "of the United States Secret Service. I suppose the Department has advised you that I would be in here this evening."

The little man jumped up at that.

"Ah, yes!" he said. "I have just gotten a telegram. Have a chair."

He thrust the telegram across the table towards Mooney, went around, and closed the door.

I could see Mooney smile as he read the telegram.

It was marked from Washington and advised the sheriff that an agent of the United States Secret Service would call on him some time this afternoon. It named this agent as Inspector Jarvis. It requested the sheriff to regard the communication as confidential in every respect, and to be governed by the wishes of the agent. It was signed by the Department of Justice.

This was a telegram that Mooney had written out on the train and which it was White's business to send by cutting the wire.

It was possible, of course, that Mooney could have impersonated an agent of the Secret Service, but it was far safer to have this impersonation preceded by a telegram from Washington. Mooney believed that the average officer, in a small locality, would be absolutely convinced by such a telegram, and that it would not occur to him to verify it—which was, in fact, the case.

The procedure was precisely what this sheriff imagined the government would follow if it wished his assistance in any matter. It would send a telegram, directly to him, naming the agent and the time of his arrival.

When the man came back from closing the door, Mooney at once began his explanation.

He said that the government had information to the effect that a gang of train robbers, who had been operating through the country, intended to hold up the express that passed west over the line that night at 1:30. The holdup would be attempted at the coal tipple west of this town where the engine stopped. He said it was impossible to be certain about this information—such sources of information were necessarily not wholly reliable— nevertheless, there was fairly good reason to believe that such an attempt would be undertaken.

He said that the Department was extremely anxious to round up these bandits who had so far eluded capture. A plan had been determined on, which he wished to carry out with the aid of the sheriff.

He then explained what he intended to do.

He said that the point of attack by the train robbers would be the express car. He did not wish the sheriff, or any posse, to take part in the effort to capture these outlaws; untrained men in an undertaking of this kind would be of little use. The employment of such persons usually resulted in someone being killed.

He would have two Secret Service men—he indicated me, and added that the other would arrive on the midnight express; the train to be held up.

He wanted the sheriff to come with him to the train.

He wished the conductor and the train officials to be impressed with the fact that the Department of Justice was very anxious to effect the capture of the men who might undertake to hold up the train at the coal tipple, and to realize the necessity of following, precisely, the directions which the Secret Service had outlined for this undertaking.

He said he would be glad if the sheriff would take charge of the express messenger and hold his force, in reserve, to come to the assistance of the Secret Service men if it should be necessary. He said it might happen that the Department's information was incorrect, or it might happen that for some reason the highwaymen would not undertake to hold up the express on this night. In which event it was of the utmost importance for every move in this affair to be kept absolutely secret. If it were told, or found its way into the newspapers, the gang of outlaws would discover the plan which the Department of Justice had undertaken for their capture.

It was now about seven o'clock.

Mooney said he would go over to the hotel, get supper, and sleep until the train came in. He would depend upon the sheriff to call at the hotel for him about half an hour before the arrival of the train.

That is the substance of Mooney's conversation with the sheriff.

He had assumed a decided, rather abrupt manner, as of one accustomed to being obeyed, and whose orders were to the point and accurate. The sheriff promised to carry out his directions precisely, as he wished, and we left his office and went over to the hotel.

We had supper and afterwards went up to our room. I was outwardly calm enough, I suppose, but inside of me every nerve was on edge. There were two beds in the room. Mooney advised me to go to sleep, as we would certainly be up all night.

To me sleep was out of the question.

But my extraordinary companion lay down on the bed and in a very short time was asleep; he continued to sleep up to the moment at which the sheriff knocked on the door.

I sat by the window for a long time and looked out at the little town and the hills beyond it until the night descended; then I lay down on one of the beds. But I did not sleep.

I had not understood the plan upon which Mooney had determined. I had seen him writing something on the train which he gave to White, and I knew that White had a telegraphic instrument, but I did not know the other details. The opening of this adventure was now becoming clear to me. But what further plan Mooney expected to carry out, I could not imagine.

The sheriff came for us at about half-past eleven, and we went over to the railroad station. The man was very mysterious. The gravity of the matter in which he had been asked to take part greatly affected the sheriff. He felt the weight of responsibility and his importance. The government had called upon him to assist it in one of those secret undertakings about which he had always conjectured, and now, at the opening of this adventure, he could not wholly conceal his concern.

It was only a short distance to the station; nevertheless, the sheriff had brought a hack, with a negro driver, to convey us.

When the train pulled in, the sheriff went at once to find the conductor. A moment later an extraordinary conference took place. The sheriff introduced Mooney to the conductor and showed his telegram from the Department of Justice.

Mooney did not give the conductor opportunity to think very much about the matter.

He said it was important for the endeavor to be kept as secret as possible, as it might fail, and the government might wish to attempt it in some other direction. He explained to the conductor as he had explained to the sheriff, that the Secret Service was not entirely certain about its information, and that the undertaking was in a certain sense precautionary; nevertheless, nothing must be neglected that might insure its success.

He pointed out that the fewest possible persons ought to be permitted to know anything about it; that the train should go on, precisely on its schedule; that nothing must be done to give any official an idea of what was in hand; and, of course, no passengers on the train must have any information as to what was about to take place. The stop at this station was one of the briefest, and Mooney hurried everybody into the train.

White, who had come on this train, now joined us, and Mooney explained to the conductor what course he wished to pursue. The plan of the Department was to effect the capture of the men who would undertake to hold up the train at the coal tipple. He pointed out that these bandits would enter the express car, as it was the sealed express against which their endeavor would be directed. He said that he, and his two men, would take charge of the express car, that the express agent should go to the rear of the train and act with the sheriff as a reserve force. In this difficult matter he preferred to have with him only the trained Secret Service men, who were accustomed to things of this sort. He said the express agent, or untrained persons, would be of no benefit to him; they, in fact, constituted a menace.

When the train moved out of the station the whole party went forward to the express car.

The sheriff and conductor explained the matter to the express agent, and introduced Mooney. Strange as it may seem, the express agent was less astonished than any of the others had been. He was aware of the holdups that had taken place throughout the country and he was, in fact, expecting something of the sort to happen. He had a short riot pump gun lying on the top of the safe and a big Colt revolver in his pocket.

Mooney here took charge of the matter without any further consultation with anybody. He told the express agent to go to the rear of the train with the sheriff. They were not to do anything unless they received a signal from Mooney.

This was the plan and it was immediately put into effect by Mooney.

But before the express agent left the car Mooney told him that he wanted to place a package of marked bills in the safe. It might happen, by some accident, that the bandits attacking the train would get the best of it. In such event the package of marked bills would serve in tracking them down. He said this precaution had been determined upon by the Department in all cases.

He produced an envelope—a brown manila envelope—sealed and stamped with red wax, and handed it to the express agent. The agent squatted down by the safe, opened it quickly, and put the envelope in among the other packages; then he closed the safe and locked it.

This device gave Mooney the combination to the safe.

He was standing close beside the express agent, stooping over with the envelope in his hand, so that it could be placed in the safe when the door was open, and he was therefore able to observe precisely what turns were made on the dial. For one with the skill of this extraordinary man, a glance was enough. When the express agent had swung the door back, Mooney knew every detail of the combination precisely.

The man now left the car.

Mooney fastened the door and proceeded at his leisure. He had explained to the sheriff that the small black leather bag which he carried contained handcuffs and weapons for his men. But it in fact contained a variety of quite different articles.

He now opened it and sat down before the safe.

The bag contained drills which Mooney had intended to use if the safe proved to be equipped with a modern time lock; as it was, these implements were not required. It also held a plumber's candle, a tube of liquid glue, and a bundle of newspapers.

He opened the safe without any difficulty whatever, for he had the combination directly from the express agent.

Inside of the safe were a number of sealed packages in large envelopes. These envelopes were not only sealed with the gummed-down flap, but they were also sealed with wax. Mooney removed all of them. He lighted the plumber's candle and very carefully held the wax seals close to the flame until they were soft enough for him to slip a knife blade under them.

When the wax seals on the packages were all thus softened and lifted up without being broken, he opened the envelopes by rolling the point of a pencil carefully along under the flap. There were quite a number of these envelopes, all consigned to one bank and, while they all contained new currency, the men were astonished to discover that this currency was in small bills.

The whole of it was in one-and two-dollar bills. There was not a bill of any larger denomination in the whole consignment.

It was possible, of course, if these men were acting on information, that the persons forwarding that information to them knew this train would carry a consignment of money but did not know the value of that consignment. They may have estimated the value of it by its bulk.

From the big stack of sealed envelopes, we all imagined that we had now made the great haul always expected. But, while the volume of currency was large, the actual value was in fact small; not, at the farthest, above a thousand or fifteen hundred dollars.

Mooney cursed as the denominations of these bills continued to appear in the packages. But there was nothing to do but go ahead. And he carried it out, in every detail, precisely as he had planned it. He removed the money from the envelopes, and packed it into his bag. Then he filled the envelopes with newspaper until they appeared to be the same bulk.

He had not enough newspaper for all the packages and we looked about the car for anything we could find for the purpose.

When the envelopes were filled with paper so they resembled, in bulk, their former appearance, Mooney gummed down the flaps and pasted down the sealing-wax seals. The packages were now all precisely in appearance as they had been when they were taken out of the safe. The seals were not broken because they had been thoroughly softened by the heat of the plumber's candle before they had been removed, and so were easily gummed back into position.

This was all carefully done. No one could have told that the packages had been in any sense tampered with. Mooney had noted the exact position they occupied in the safe, and he returned them precisely to this position.

The envelope, which he had given the express agent to put in with them, he also restored to the position it had occupied when the agent thrust it in. He had plenty of leisure to carry this out unhurriedly. It had all been accomplished by the time the train arrived at the coal tipple.

Mooney closed the safe. The train stopped to take coal and went on.

The sheriff, the nervous conductor, and the armed express agent waited in vain for the signal to bring them forward into a desperate encounter with outlaws.

When the train pulled out Mooney opened the door to the express car and sent me back for the conductor and his associates.

They came immediately and Mooney acted out the last scene in his comedy.

He told the men that the Department's information about the holdup at this tipple had been probably intended as misleading. One never knew whether one had precisely any criminal plan. This information may have been given out to the Department with the primary intention of leading it to look for the train robbers at a point distant from that at which they were intending to put their criminal operations into effect.

He directed everybody, by order of the Department of Justice, to say nothing about this matter. All were warned, under no circumstances, to say anything about it, no matter if there should be an investigation on account of the robbery having taken place at some other point. The United States Secret Service had put into effect here, on this train, a plan upon which it was accustomed to depend, and this plan must not become public.

The man's nerve and assurance were without limit.

When he had finished, he requested the express agent to return to him the dummy package of marked bills which he had given him to put into the safe. Any one else in the world would have hesitated to have the safe opened, and would either have removed the dummy envelope when he took out the packages of money, or would have left it; but not Mooney. He had set out to do every detail in this undertaking with precision and order, and he did not intend to leave any item unaccomplished.

The express agent opened the safe, took out the envelope, gave it to him, and locked the safe again. And at the next station we shook hands with everybody and got down.

We took a through train east, having carried out what I felt at the time, and what I now feel, to have been a criminal adventure of unequaled assurance. So successful was it that we never heard anything more about it. Nothing concerning it was ever published or made known so far as I have been able to find out.

The robbery, of course, appeared when the packages of currency were delivered at the bank. But nobody knew at what place this robbery had been accomplished; whether it was done at the point of shipment, some place along the line, or where the packages were delivered to the banks.

It was likely that neither the sheriff nor any of the train officials ever said anything about the government agent who took charge of the express car on that night. There was no reason for them to give any information.

Was it not the work of the United States Secret Service? And had they not been warned to silence?

CHAPTER V

THE BIG HAUL

It was a soft October night with a bare threat of frost in the air; the sky gray with stars, and a vast silence.

Three men were lying out before a fire of tree limbs in a forest. It was a country of mountains, the foothills of the Alleghenies extending westward toward the Ohio. In every direction were wooded hills, the rough mountainous foothills of the great range as it broke down westward toward the flat lands.

For some reason that I do not know, Mooney was confident that he had finally located the treasure train for which he had been always looking.

As I have said before, in this narrative, I did not know what sources of information were available to this man, but I think he had some cue to what was being shipped. At any rate he was confident that, at last, he was about to make "the great haul."

We had come into this country together and had got off at a town some fifty miles distant from the point at which we were now lying before our wood fire. From this town we had each taken a different train to a station in the direction of the place at which Mooney intended to make the holdup. I had gone to a station farthest along the line; from the two other stations, Mooney and White had walked along the track until they picked me up. We came finally to the water tank in the mountains, at which point Mooney had determined to hold up the New York & St. Louis Express.

He knew all about this train; knew that it stopped at this water tank in the mountains on schedule time, and knew what it carried on this night.

We had all gone about a mile and a half east of the tank where a small stream came down out of the mountain. We had followed this stream perhaps a quarter of a mile into the wood and there we had built the fire.

At midnight we got up and followed the little stream down to the track; here we divided; White was to go about two miles west along the track, while Mooney and I were to take up a position in the shadow of the water tank.

We were barely in position, in the heavy shadow, when I heard the train; it seemed far off, a low rumble in the mountains. Then suddenly it thundered through a gap in the hills and pulled up by the tank. It required only a few moments to take water, and as the train pulled out Mooney and I slipped from the heavy shadow and swung up on the rear of the tender.

We climbed very quickly down towards the engine cab.

Here I very nearly had a serious accident. I caught hold of something in the darkness which looked like a hand rail. It proved to be a rake used by the fireman, and it was hot. The inside of my hand was scorched. I made some exclamation unconsciously indicating that my hand was burned. The fireman and engineer both turned toward us.

They were met by Mooney, the black mask over his face and a pistol in his hand.

I had recovered myself and stood now beside him, also masked and with a weapon. It was the old form of mask which Mooney had invented; attached to the inside of the hat and loaded with shot to hold it down. The men in the engine cab made no resistance. The fireman merely stood with his mouth open, like a child before a ghost. The engineer had some composure.

"Don't shoot," he said; "what's the order?"

Mooney told the engineer to stop opposite a fire he would see on the right hand side of the track about a mile further on. With the pistol at his temple the engineer was not slow to obey this direction. Mooney had told White to build a fire beside the track when he reached the point about two miles west.

White had suggested a flash light as being better for this purpose.

But Mooney said there was always a possibility of a wrecking train, or some special, passing, and if so, the man with the flash light would stop the wrong train, but if it were a fire, built in the woods, a passing train would give it no attention, as merely a hobo camp.

White had followed his direction and we presently pulled up by the fire. Mooney left me to guard the engineer while he took the fireman in front of him and went down the side of the train. He made the fireman cut the train in two back of the mail car.

I stood in the door of the cab with my weapon on the engineer. I knew when the train had been cut, and, as Mooney had directed me, I ordered the engineer to pull forward for fifty yards and stop. Mooney sent the fireman back to the rear of the train after the mail car had been uncoupled, then he went forward and joined White.

The two men took the clerks out of the mail car; they selected the chief clerk, then they sent the remainder of the mail clerks to the rear of the train. There was a touch of thoughtfulness in Mooney's consideration for these men; there was a chill of frost in the air and he told them to put on their coats before they went out into the night.

When these men had gone back to the rear of the train, Mooney, White, and the chief clerk got into the mail car, then they signaled the engineer to move ahead. I understood the signal and when the engineer paid no attention to it I spoke to him as roughly as I could.

"Go ahead," I said, "until you are stopped with the air signal."

He pulled the train out without a word, and when he got the air signal he stopped.

Here Mooney left White in the car with the clerk and got down on the ground in order to keep watch for any one who might be coming. I learned afterwards precisely what happened in that car. The clerk made some objections and Mooney spoke to him from the darkness before the open door:

"Friend," he said, "you are steppin' on a trigger."

It was the end of every form of hesitation.

The man pointed out the mail sacks at once. White cut the straps and dumped the contents on the floor. He found a lot of securely sealed packages which he knew from experience contained money. Tearing open the corners of a few of them he discovered that they were bank notes. He spoke to Mooney who now came up to the door of the car.

White was amazed; he realized that they had found the long-looked-for big haul.

They selected one of the light mail sacks and put the packages into it. Mooney then came forward to the engine. White sent the mail clerk back down the track. Mooney now took charge of the engineer.

He made him pull down the track for perhaps half a mile, then he stopped and put him off. He ran the engine, himself, for perhaps a mile farther, then stopped again. White and I got out of the train and Mooney gave the engine just enough steam at the throttle so that it would move off slowly and stop a mile or so farther on, then he swung down on the ground and joined us. He did not open the throttle of the engine for he knew that on the twisting road through the mountain the train might go off the track on the sharp curves.

It was his policy never to do unnecessary damage. He did not wish to wreck the train or cause the possible wreck of any other train traveling in the night.

We turpentined our shoes, and started in a due line north by west toward a town on the Ohio River. We traveled all night. When daylight appeared we stopped and hid ourselves in the mountains. Here, Mooney and White opened the mail sack and examined the packages of money.

They had one hundred and two thousand dollars in bank notes.

But it was not in the form of such bank notes as one is accustomed to see. The notes were in sheets and unsigned, in the form that the United States Treasury is accustomed to send currency to the national banks.

This discovery did not seem to impress Mooney but it put White in despair.

For a long time Mooney said nothing; finally he took White to one side and talked with him; presently they came back to me. He showed me the sheets of notes and pointed out that they could not be used. They lacked the signatures of the bank officers and an attempt to pass them would lead immediately to one's arrest.

They determined now to hide the money and go on.

It was necessary to put it in some place where it would not be open to the rain. For this purpose they looked about for a hollow tree. Finally they found a chestnut on the wooded ridge of the hill. They put the mail sack into the hollow of this tree—crowding it up tightly so that it would not fall down—then they skillfully filled the hollow of the tree with leaves and a few broken branches, removing with care every trace of their work.

We went on.

We slept during the day, in the leaves, hidden by a tree top or covered by a log and traveled at night. It was a long tiresome journey. We carried provisions for three days. We had a compass, flash lights, and a map; but it was heavy traveling in the night, over the ridges of hills, across ravines, and through the dense undergrowth of the valleys.

Finally, we came out before the town on the Ohio. Here Mooney handed me five hundred dollars and told me to return to the circus; giving me the name of the town for which I should purchase a ticket at the station.

I never saw either of the two men again.

But I learned afterward what happened to them.

It was by no means the intention of these two men to abandon this fortune in bank notes.

They brought the money in after I was gone. White went into the town and bought a big traveling bag in a pawnshop. They put the notes into it and checked it to a city in the southwest. But first Mooney examined the notes, taking down the names of the national banks to which they were consigned.

Then they made a rather extended tour together.

They went to the cities in which these national banks were located and picked up there bills issued by the banks; this gave them the signatures their money required.

Mooney showed White how to get the signatures on the currency.

He used a simple and ingenious method. He placed the bill of which he wished to take off the signature on a piece of glass about 3 x 6 inches. He procured a pasteboard box and cut a hole in it somewhat larger than the length and width of the signature; then he placed the glass with the bill on it over this hole. He then laid a piece of white paper over the glass and put a high candlepower light inside the box. It was then an easy matter to trace the signature he wanted on the white paper.

They then made a rubber stamp of the signature; making first a steel etching of the traced signature and after that the stamp. They then cut the bills, stamped them with the proper signatures, divided the money and separated.

It seemed that the two men were not of one mind about the risk that would follow the use of this money. Each adhered to his own judgment. They were agreed upon one thing, that having made their great haul, this form of criminal adventure was ended. They were through with train hold-ups. They had each some fifty thousand dollars in currency.

After having divided the money, Mooney followed the old plan of trusting his share of it in the traveling bag. He checked it to another point farther into the southwest, while White remained where he was.

I am going to tell you what happened to White.

This daring robbery, with the loss of the big consignment of bank notes of the Treasury, produced immense excitement in the country.

At two o'clock on the night of the holdup, the conductor in charge of this train reported from the first telegraph office that he could reach, that his train had been held up one mile west of that point, by masked men who compelled the members of the crew, except the chief mail clerk and engineer, to get off, and cut the mail car from the rest of the train, taking it west with the engine.

The chief clerk returned at three o'clock in the morning and reported that the robbers had stopped and compelled him and the engineer to get off. They had then taken the engine and car farther west.

At 3:00 o'clock the engineer reported that he was on his way west looking for the engine.

At 4:15 o'clock he called from a way station, saying that he had found the engine and would come back at once for the rest of the train.

Immediately special trains were sent out, taking United States Marshals, the sheriffs of neighboring counties, officers, and bloodhounds. In a very short time Secret Service men, post-office inspectors, and all the best experts in the service of the government were on the scene.

But they were totally unable to discover anything.

The turpentine which we had used made the use of the bloodhounds of no benefit to the detectives, and it was not possible to discover the point at which we had left the engine and mail car. Nevertheless the search was not abandoned.

It extended itself now in wider directions.

The banks throughout the country were notified of the serial numbers of this currency; and the thing which Mooney, wiser than White, foresaw, presently occurred. A clearing house in the southwestern city to which White had gone, notified the Treasury Department at Washington that one of these serial numbers had passed through.

The Treasury Department acted at once.

It sent two officials to this city to run the matter down. These men were careful, experienced and able detectives. They set on foot every investigation which seemed likely to have any result; but they were not able to discover the source of the note which had been observed by the clearing house.

But they remained in charge of the undertaking.

Finally fortune favored them. One day, a young girl came in to the post office to deposit part of her salary at the Postal Savings window. A bill which she offered was of the serial numbers of the stolen currency. The post-office clerk who had been instructed to look out for these numbers immediately called the two government detectives to the window.

When questioned, the girl said she had gotten this bill from a machinery company as part of her salary.

The two detectives went to this company.

They found that this particular note had been brought in by one of their drivers who had received it from a man named White. They discovered that this man White had a machine shop in the city.

They did not at once undertake to interview White.

They shadowed the machine shop until they had an opportunity to get very careful observations of White. They had little data to go on, but they thought he was about the size of one of the bandits described by the mail clerks.

They examined the names attached to the note and finally determined they had been made with a rubber stamp. They, then, interviewed all the local stamp dealers, but could find no one who had any knowledge of such a stamp.

However, they remained in the city and continued to shadow White.

They followed him from place to place, and wherever he made purchases they would go in after him and demand of the storekeeper the note which White had passed, giving another in place of it. They would, then, have the person from whom they had obtained the note write his name on it so that it could later be identified as having been received from this man White.

In this manner they finally got a number of bills bearing the serial numbers of the notes which had been taken in the train robbery. But this was all the evidence they were able to obtain.

Finally when investigations in other directions all failed to bring anything more to light, they determined to arrest White. Accordingly one day they followed him when he got on a street car at his machine shop, and when he got down, at some place of business in the city, they stepped up to him and asked him if his name was White. He said it was; they then asked him to go with them to help in regard to some forgeries. White very willingly said that he would be glad to help them in any way he could and would go if they insisted; but that he knew nothing about any forgeries.

They took him to their office in the post-office building.

Here he was searched and a roll of these lost bills found in his possession. They were all on the same bank, and, what seemed significant, their serial numbers ran consecutively.

When questioned about where he had obtained this money, White replied that he had won it in a poker game from two men who had come into his shop several days before.

The two government detectives did not believe this story.

They talked to White a long time, but his statement could not be shaken. He described the two men with whom he had played poker, gave in detail their inquiries about some work they wished done at his shop, pointing out the exact time at which the thing occurred, and how the poker game had been led up to. He did not know the names of the two men, but gave precisely their description.

The two government detectives remained unconvinced and they determined upon an old experiment.

They took White to jail and locked him into a cell. Then they went out, returned by the rear entrance and placed themselves where they could watch the man in the cell. Here White, now very much concerned, fell unconsciously into habits which he had acquired in similar surroundings. He put his hands behind him and began to pace up and down the cell—three steps down, three steps up, slowly, back and forth—his head dropped forward in reflection.

The two government detectives watched him for a few minutes, then they went out. They decided that White must have a penitentiary record somewhere on account of his actions in the cell. The two detectives went down to the telegraph office and sent a message to every penitentiary in the United States, giving an accurate description of White, and the holdup in which they believed him to have taken part. They received a reply from the warden of a penitentiary in the northwest, saying that a man answering that description had served time for train robbery.

The detectives now determined to take White north for trial.

On this trip White escaped from the custody of the officials. The manner of his escape was extraordinarily clever. It was done without a struggle of any character. White simply disappeared.

The two detectives were traveling with White in the stateroom of a pullman. The design of these staterooms is familiar to every one. On the right of the entrance door is a couch running the full length of the side of the room. On the immediate left is the lavatory and next to that, also on the left, are the two double seats facing each other across a small aisle. White sat next to the window on the first seat beside a guard. The two government detectives were on the couch facing White.

About ten o'clock at night and just before the train pulled into a station, one of the government detectives went out into the car to look up a porter in order to have the berths made up for the night. As he left the stateroom, the other detective arose and stood in the open door.

White, who had been sitting apparently asleep, got up slowly, yawned, extended his arms and started leisurely toward the lavatory door. The main door to the stateroom stood open. It was hinged to swing inward and when so open covered the door to the lavatory. This door to the stateroom was now about half open and the government detective was standing in the door.

White had barely space enough to pass behind this door in order to reach the lavatory, but he edged himself deliberately through without arousing the slightest suspicion. Before the government detective could step around the stateroom door in order to follow White, he had entered the lavatory, slammed the door and locked it.

The government detective, now alarmed, began to beat on the steel door and demand that White open it.

He received no answer, and, as it was impossible to break in the door, he ordered the train stopped. Leaving the guard before the door of the stateroom the two government detectives now jumped down from either end of the car. These two men hurried toward each other along the side of the car on which the stateroom was located. But they found no sign of White. They then discovered that White had made his way through the small window in the lavatory and dropped off the moving train.

The authorities had now a definite description of White.

This they put out over the country, and another great man hunt began. It was the theory of the officials that White, like any other criminal who was being sought after, would at once undertake to leave the country. White knew this and he determined upon precisely the reverse of this course. He selected the most conspicuous and consequently the very last place that detectives on the search for a criminal would be likely to look.

They were finally able to trace him to Cincinnati. They had his photograph and thousands of circulars were struck off from it and posted in every depot and public place in the country; sent out broadcast to every city and every federal officer. The clew in Cincinnati mysteriously vanished.

But this man, clever and resourceful, was not fated to escape.

One day a medical student in a college in the middle west called on the local post-office inspector. He said that he had seen the poster describing White, which had been placed all over the country and had observed the resemblance to a fellow student in the college. There was a reward of $1000, and he wished to obtain this reward. The student studied the description given in the poster. One of the items of description was that the man wanted had a split thumb nail. The student waited for an opportunity to observe his suspected associate's thumb. He found that the man's hand corresponded to the description; "ridge extending the full length of the thumb nail on the left hand ... the thumb nail has evidently been split open and the ridge left as a scar ... the third finger of the left hand is somewhat crooked and stiff."

The government authorities were at once notified by the post-office inspector. The suspected student was shadowed, identified as White and arrested.

He was brought north; this time attended with every precaution and handcuffed to a guard. Here he was tried for the robbery, convicted and sentenced to twenty-five years in the penitentiary.

Thus closed the career of White. The finish of Mooney was more adventurous and spectacular.

CHAPTER VI

THE PASSING OF MOONEY

A strange fatality seemed to follow White and Mooney.

These two men were perhaps the most accomplished highwaymen that ever operated in any country, and yet something unforeseen—something they seemed unable to anticipate—always interfered to prevent them from obtaining the great fortune they expected.

In one of the earlier robberies, the packages done up in old newspapers which they kicked out of the way, when they were searching for the shipment of money, contained the very treasure for which they were looking; while the only thing they carried away from that night's work was an inconsiderable sum of money gathered from the rifled registered mail.

The sealed packages that Mooney took out of the safe on the night that he and I, in such theatrical fashion, held up the through express, proved, upon examination, to be registered bonds of some industrial corporation which were being delivered in the south, while the loot from the last holdup had been about a thousand dollars in small bills.

And now, finally in the great haul which they were at last able to make, the only result was White's capture and imprisonment for a term of years, equal practically, for life. The thing ended also in disaster no less for Mooney.

I have often wondered who this man really was and what was his origin.

I think he had been in nearly every country, and he was familiar with practically every device that could be of service to his profession. He was a skilled electrician; a very wizard at it. The manager of the circus was glad to carry him along although he had practically no duties. But the skill with which he was able to adjust anything of a mechanical nature that happened, for the moment, to be out of repair, made him invaluable. And he seemed to do it with no effort; with practically no preliminary inquiry, as though, by a sort of instinct, he was able to locate the difficulty and adjust it. I have always felt that given any sort of an even chance the government officials would never have been able to outwit this man. It was not any plan laid for him that tripped him up. It was the inevitable tragedy of life.

I did not think about this very much at the time. I was young enough for events to make little impression on me. The whole thing was a sort of adventure, without, as it seemed to me, any moral relations.

I traveled on for some weeks with the circus precisely as I had been accustomed to do.

I helped with the horses. My disappearance caused no comment in the organization where my status was practically that of a roustabout. I continued to adore the girl who rode the white horse, and whenever I had an opportunity I talked to her. I could not have been very skillful in dissimulation for my admiration was apparent to everybody. Maggie did not say anything to me; she never even mentioned White or Mooney, but I found her often regarding me as though I were something she did not precisely comprehend, or as though she were considering me in some plan about which she was very much concerned.

They were careless and happy days.

Strange as it may appear, I never anticipated any after affect to these adventures. I did not realize that I was in danger from the law, or that what had happened to White might on any day happen to me.

About two weeks later Maggie disappeared from the circus.

I learned the fact next morning from the girl who had been placed under the chaperonage of one of the clowns' wives, a morose wizened old woman, whose husband, the life of the circus when the performance was under way, was at all other times the most melancholy person one could imagine, and whose withered wife seemed never to escape from this depression. I learned also that the girl was not related to Maggie, as Mooney had once intimated. She had been adopted by this curious, capable woman, probably out of a hospital.

I learned afterwards what this disappearance of Maggie meant. She had received a telegram from Mooney who was involved in his last adventure.

This woman was not in any sense an accomplice of Mooney.

I think he had never seen her until he joined this circus. I am sure there was no understanding of any character between them. In his extremity, Mooney merely turned toward her as perhaps the only person he could think of.

He had been overtaken by an unforeseen misfortune.

After the bank notes had all been signed and made ready for circulation, he left White in the south. He was convinced the plan which White proposed to follow would bring him to misfortune. He pointed out very clearly what would happen, and he was right. He had no faith in White's assurance and he had no intention to submit himself to the possibility of any such disaster.

He had shipped his money to a city in the southwest and he followed it there.

I do not know whether he intended to cross into Mexico or whether he planned that the government officials who might be looking for him should finally be able to trace him in that direction, and, from this, to formulate the theory that he had crossed the southern border.

This would be quite in line with the man's character.

At any rate the fact was, that, having made this false trail toward southern territory, he turned suddenly about and came north. He brought the money with him in the traveling bag. But here in a northern city he was overtaken by a misfortune which no man could foresee and to which all are subject, no matter how wily or skillful.

He was taken desperately ill and he realized his condition immediately. He took the traveling bag to an express company and shipped it to Canada to a fictitious person. Then he looked about for a lodging house. He was afraid to go to a hospital; and, yet, from what Maggie afterward said, Mooney was even then, in the first few hours of his illness, certain that he had reached the end of his career.

The man had no difficulty in finding what he was looking for; but here he was met with one of those inexplicable vagaries of chance for which there seems to be no adequate explanation.

It was night when Mooney got out of the cab and was helped into the lodging which he had selected. In the preoccupation of his illness he did not very closely regard the person who maintained this lodging house. But in the morning when the man came up to the room Mooney knew him instantly.

Years before in a holdup in which Mooney had been engaged there had been a German mail clerk. More than once when Mooney had been in the mood of reminiscence I had heard him talk about this ridiculous person; a pale mild-mannered German, who had been simply unnerved with terror when the bandit had entered the mail car. This man had been physically unable, from sheer fright, to get down out of the car when the mail clerks at the point of a weapon had been ordered out.

He sat on the floor with his mouth open and his hands clasped together.

Mooney used to laugh about it; about the ridiculous appearance the creature presented and what he had done. He had pulled an empty mail sack down over the man's head and shoulders and left him there; and there he had been found three hours later when the train pulled into one of the central cities of the west. The German had not moved and the mail sack was still pulled down over his shoulders when the train men at the station came into the car.

The man had been laughed out of the service and had gone from one undertaking to another, until, finally, destiny established him here in this boarding house to meet Mooney when he should arrive ill in a hired cab.

Mooney, as I have said, knew the man instantly, but it was not likely that the man recognized the awe-inspiring bandit in his sick lodger. But he looked at Mooney as at some person whom he had seen, and the highwayman knew that it was only a question of time until his host would be able to place him.

The impressions of fright are conspicuously vivid.

It was certain that this man's mind retained the precise picture of the one who had put him into such abject terror. The picture would be clear in every detail. Time does not blur impressions like this. It would be merely a question of the mental connecting up of his impressions about this lodger whom, he felt, he had seen somewhere, and the identity of the highwayman who had put him so desperately into fear.

It was then that Mooney sent the telegram to Maggie. He got the German to take it out to the telegraph office, and he awaited her arrival. He did not send for a doctor. He knew perfectly well that death was on him. He had contracted the swift deadly pneumonia which at that time was devastating the country like a plague.

Maggie reached the city that evening and Mooney told her what to do. He pointed out that the German lodging-house keeper had already hit upon his identity and the house was being watched, for he had noticed a window across the street, back of a barber shop, that always had the shade pulled down. The window was visible from his bed and he could see, by watching it, that this shade moved occasionally.

He observed it closely and at one time saw a man's hand, which was all the evidence a person like Mooney needed. He knew perfectly well that the German had recognized him and reported the fact to the police.

He explained it all to Maggie when she came in. She knew then that she would be shadowed when she went out of the house. He told her, precisely, what he wished her to do.

It was about five o'clock in the afternoon.

Maggie presently left the house and was of course shadowed. She went along the street until she came to a doctor's office. She rang the bell and entered. This destination seemed reasonable to the plain-clothes man who was keeping her in sight. This was precisely what one summoned to the bedside of an ill man would be expected to do; go at once for a physician.

But it was not a doctor that Maggie was after.

It was an opportunity to call up the office of the express company in Canada and tell them to ship the bag back to this city. If the doctor were in, she would consult him about Mooney and ask to use his telephone, and if he were not in she would ask the same privilege, saying that she would return when the doctor should be at home.

As it happened the doctor was not in the house, but the person in charge of his office permitted Maggie to use the telephone. She called up the express company in Canada and ordered the bag reshipped. She left with the servant money to pay for the telephone call and went out.

It was a very clever device because it did not occur to the detective, who was keeping her in sight, that it was worth while to go into the doctor's office to inquire what she was doing there.

What she would be doing there was too obvious.

He therefore contented himself with shadowing her back to the lodging house and keeping the place under his eye from the curtained window behind the barber shop.

Maggie remained with the sick man that night. She endeavored in vain to persuade him to have a doctor or to permit her to undertake such simple remedies as might be at hand. Mooney knew he was dying. He had no faith whatever in anything that might be done for him.

He was only concerned that Maggie should carry out his directions.

In the morning she again left the house; and was again shadowed as every one was shadowed who came into it or went out of it. This time Maggie went to the nearest drug store—about three blocks distant, at the corner of a street—went in, spoke to the clerk and then went around the counter into the back part of the store.

The detective who was watching her from the opposite side of the street naturally concluded she was having some remedy prepared for the sick man.

What Maggie had in fact done was to say to the clerk that she was packing up some articles, which she had to move, and that she wanted to get some empty boxes. The boxes were in the rear of the store and the clerk told her she could go through and pick out what she wished. She went through, went out the back door, down a neighboring alley and took a taxicab to the railway station.

The detective waited in vain for her to appear. When finally she did not come out he went in and discovered what had happened; too late to overtake her.

Maggie went to the station, got the traveling bag, put it into the taxicab and set about to carry out the remainder of Mooney's directions.

The detective called up headquarters and gave the alarm. The police at once went about spreading the usual net for Maggie and then they determined to arrest Mooney. They were now convinced that the man's illness was a pretense; and, a few minutes later, the detective and three officers suddenly burst into the room where Mooney sat in bed propped up with pillows, gasping for breath, in the closing stages of pneumonia.

Mooney was painfully writing something on the blank sheet of a letter pad with a stump of a pencil.

The officers covered him with weapons.

Mooney looked at them with a queer, ghastly smile:

"You are in time," he said, "to witness my will."

He extended his arm with the sheet of paper in his fingers.

The astonished officers took the paper to the window and read it in amazement.

It ran as follows:

"I, John Mooney, being at the end of life, do hereby make this my last will and testament.

"Inasmuch as the United States Government, with a tender regard beyond that of friend or relative, has, now for a long time, been extremely solicitous to provide me with food, clothing and the necessities of life:

"Now, therefore, in appreciative remembrance, I do, by these Presents, give and bequeath to the said United States Government fifty-one thousand dollars in bank notes, which I have caused on this day to be delivered to the Federal District Attorney of this city;

"In the hope that the said United States Government, having thus esteemed me in life, may now, in death, cherish my memory.

(Signed) "John Mooney."

They realized now that the man was in the very extremity of death. He was dying as he had lived, with a cynical disregard of everybody. His very last words were in character:

"Tell 'em—no flowers."

His voice was a gasping stutter.

In the meantime Maggie had gone to the railroad station, found the traveling bag which had been reshipped, and had taken a taxicab to the office of the District Attorney; precisely as Mooney had directed in his will.

But there she had not carried out his directions in its exact details.

I would like to write into this record that it was Mooney, on his deathbed, who thought of the course that Maggie followed, but it would not be the truth. He thought only of the cynical jest that he endeavored to carry out in his death. It was Maggie who was thinking of some one else. What she did will presently appear.

I suppose it was about a week later when a man came into the horse tent, and walked up to me as though he were an old acquaintance:

"How do you do?" he said.

His greeting was so cordial, that, although I did not know him, I put out my hand to shake hands with him. But instead of grasping my hand as I expected, he took hold of it and turned it suddenly over so he could see the palm.

There, still visible, was the red discoloration from the burn when I had taken hold of the hot iron rod, on the night when we had climbed down from the tender into the cab of the locomotive, in our last holdup.

The man seemed surprised, as though at finding some confirmatory evidence of which he had been in doubt.

He looked me over.

"You are only a boy," he said. "How did you get mixed up in this business?"

I was, myself, now astonished. I realized that the man was an officer and that I had finally, in some manner, got into the clutches of the law. It all seemed so incredible that I did not undertake to make any reply to the man's inquiry. He asked me to go with him and I put on my hat and went without a word.

The circus was on that day at a rather large city.

We took a street car to the post-office, a big, white building in the center of a public square. We got into the elevator and went up to the second floor. The man took me along a narrow hall and into a room which was entirely empty. Here he bade me wait, and went through a door into an adjoining room.

I remained for some time quite alone. The sounds of the city came up to me, but I seemed in some deserted place far from any one.

Finally the officer, who had arrested me, came back, opened the door and asked me to go in. He closed the door behind me and went out into the hall.

I found myself in a big sunlit room.

There was a table with several leather-bound books on it, some folded papers in their wrappers and some written memoranda, on sheets, lying about, and a chair where some one had just been sitting. Then I saw the other person in the room; a figure standing by the window; a big man with thick gray hair, tall and broad shouldered.

He had been looking down into the street and now he turned about; his face lighted with a friendly, quizzical smile. The smile deepened; extended itself until it became a merry chuckle.

"So you are the desperate train robber!" he said.

"Well, sit down, Mr. Train Robber, I want to have a little conversation with you."

I was as embarrassed as a child and I sat down primly in the chair and put my hands together in my lap. I must have presented a ridiculous appearance, a big overgrown boy as uneasy as though he were being photographed for his mother.

The man came over and sat down in his chair. He put his elbows on the table and looked at me across the line of books.

"Is this all really true?" he said.

"Yes, sir," I replied.

I knew of course what he meant although he made no explanation.

"Well," he said, "it is incredible; it is entirely beyond belief."

Then he got up and began to walk about the room.

"My boy," he said, "you have been associated with two of the worst crooks in the world and you have engaged in a desperate business. What do you suppose we ought to do with you?"

"I don't know," I said.

I was still greatly embarrassed and these were the only words I could think of.

The big man stopped at that, put his hands in his pockets and looked at me:

"Neither do I," he said.

Then he went on:

"You have courage—a dependable sort of courage. It is a quality rare enough in the world; too rare, it seems to me, to be thoughtlessly broken up. I am going to try an experiment.

"I don't see why the courage which you possess should not be brought to the service of the government instead of against it. Do you think you could stick to us as faithfully as you have stuck to these two inconsiderate blacklegs?"

He did not wait for me to reply; but he went on:

"Crime always fails," he said. "There never was any man able to get away with it. No matter how clever he is, there is always some point at which his plans go to pieces; sooner or later something turns up against which he is wholly unable to protect himself. The thing is so certain to happen that it seems to look as though there were a power in the universe determined on the maintenance of justice; a power that is opposed to criminal endeavor and always at work to destroy the criminal agent—just as it destroyed White and just as it has destroyed Mooney."

He went on as though he were speaking to himself.

"But it does not act as though it wished to destroy you.... I suppose one's large view in this matter ought to be consistent. If one assumes that this Authority has exercised itself for the ultimate destruction of these two hardened offenders, then one must also believe that what has happened in your behalf has happened also with an equal design."

He began to walk about the room, his hands in his pockets, his chin lifted as in some reflection.

"Well," he said, "at any rate I am going to take it that way. I am going to turn you over to Dix for a tryout in the Secret Service. We have got to seize a number of dangerous Reds and your holdup experience ought to make you a useful assistant for Dix. Besides," he added, "we are involved in a sort of promise about you."

I said "Yes, sir."

I was still embarrassed and astonished almost beyond any expression; and, sitting thus primly on the edge of the chair, with my big hands folded in my lap, I must have seemed to the man irresistibly ridiculous, for he suddenly began to laugh.

"All right, Mr. Train Robber," he said, "you will find some of your friends just outside of the door, and when you have spoken with them, go along the hall to the end of the building.... Dix is in the room on the right."

I got up awkwardly and backed out of the room and through the door behind me.

It was only long afterwards that I learned by what agency these events had come to pass.

When Maggie had taken the traveling bag containing the stolen bank notes to the United States District Attorney on the day of Mooney's death, she had not handed them over to him, straight out, as Mooney had directed. Instead, she had used the advantages of the situation to bring me clear of the business.

I do not know the details.

But she seems to have gone over the whole thing with the Federal authorities that morning, explaining all about my relations with the two highwaymen, how I had come to get into it and how I had been carried along; and then she promised to deliver the money to them provided the government would grant me immunity. The matter was taken up and discussed there in detail on that morning. The result was that Maggie got the promise, that, if everything proved to be as she described it, I should not be held responsible for the desperate crimes that these men had carried out.

She was in fact a very skillful person and she conducted it with immense cleverness.

They were amazed to find that she had the money in what they imagined, when she came, was merely a personal traveling bag. And they were astonished to discover that I was, in fact, merely the big awkward, thoughtless youth that she had described to them; as they were astonished to find the confirmatory discoloration of my burned hand.

On the outside of the door I found Maggie and my fairy sweetheart.

The girl was in tears, but Maggie was a grim figure, with her little crumpled ears lying tight to her head, her beady eyes and her hard features—precisely like the devil, which she was not.

"You can kiss her, just once!" she said.

I stood like one in a dream, but the girl came up and put her arms around my neck ... and I kissed her.

And then, through the rosy haze of the world, Maggie pushed in between us.

"That'll do," she said. "You are to go to work now and make a man out of yourself ... and then ... in three years we shall see about it."

I went along the corridor, to Dix ... in the room on the right.

* * * *

And so came Walker into the United States Secret Service. The story of his way upward in that service is not written out here. If you wish to hear it ask his charming wife whose memories go back to the time when the big tent of a circus was the Kingdom of Romance. But you will find in the chapters to follow, some adventures in mystery with which he was connected.

CHAPTER VII

THE DIAMOND

The thing that keeps life keen is that you can never figure out what's ahead.

There's always a surprise around the corner. The thing changes on you, to use an expression of the vernacular. One begins in an English drawing-room and winds up on the Gobi Desert. You never know where the road's going. Take it in big things, or take it in the trivialities of life—it's the same system.

But I am not going to lecture on philosophy; I am going to cite a case—a case that had an immense surprise in it to me, and a series of events that started out in one direction and concluded in another. I saw them start simply enough, but they "changed on me," to keep our colloquialism.

I had just come down from Bar Harbor. I had an artificial diamond made in Germany, and I was looking for Walker. Walker is chief of the United States Secret Service, and he knows more about artificial stones than any other man in America, unless it is Bartoldi.

Gems are a fad with Walker, and a profession with Bartoldi.

I do not know which of these motive impulses moves a man to the higher efficiency. The keen man with the fad gets to be an expert, and the necessities of trade makes the other one. Anyway, I wanted to show my diamond to both of them.

I found Walker in the Forty-seventh National Bank on lower Fifth Avenue. He waved a recognition and went on with what he was saying to the cashier behind the grill:

"There was no robbery; that's what puzzles me. How did they get the thing? It's lucky the bank discovered that it was missing almost immediately and sent out the word. The package had just come in, and was lying on a shelf under the bookkeeper's desk.... But how did they get it?"

And so I found Walker.

Nobody would ever have taken Walker for the chief of the government Secret Service. In appearance he was the last person any one would have picked out for a secret agent.

He looked like a practical person, and that is precisely what he was. You never could think that the man had any imagination; and he didn't have any. At least, he didn't have any imagination in the sense that we usually understand it. I suppose he had the kind of imagination that the inventor has, or the mathematician when he figures the orbit of the stars, or the engineer when he has to make some calculation on the stresses of a bridge.

I asked him to look at my diamond when he came out. His face took on a decided expression of interest.

"Go up and see Bartoldi," he said. "I will be along in an hour."

He added with a sort of smile:

"There is no leisure in my trade. Somebody's always either robbing a national bank or trying to rob—boring from within or setting up some game on the outside."

Then he laughed.

Now, that is how I happened to find Walker—just when I wanted to find him. By accident I stepped into something, as you would say.

Well, it was not explained to me. In fact, to say plain truth, behind a lot of courteous indirections, he put me out of the bank and sent me up to Bartoldi's to await his coming in an hour. I do not mean that he ordered me out. He enticed me out; he edged me out, a good deal as one would do with a child that had wandered into a rather tense conference.

I went up to Bartoldi's. Everybody knows where it is.

He has a mammoth place on Fifth Avenue, rather far up—the trade is going up. The big retailers saw that a dozen years ago. Bartoldi is not the greatest jewel dealer in the world, but he is one of the greatest. The greatest jewel dealer in the world is Mahadol in Bombay; then come Vanderdick in Amsterdam, and Hauseman in Paris.

It is a big shop, as I have said. But you know it—there is no reason to describe it here. A huge place with glass cases like every American shop, and the jewels displayed, as is the almost universal custom in America. Not like some of the foreign places, where you see only a square of black velvet, and the jewel, when you have named the kind you want, is brought out of a vault.

I was in this shop before the long counter that contains the tray of diamonds, when Bartoldi appeared.

Appeared is precisely the word; I did not see him until suddenly he was before me on the other side of the glass case.

He does not look like a jeweler. In fact, he does not look like anybody in active life. He is big and gaunt, and, in spite of the best tailor, he gives one the impression of an immense human body dried out in some desert. But he is alive, all right. I would like to see the man who could fool him about a jewel.

I showed him my diamond. It was a big diamond, unset, and I had it folded up in a piece of tissue paper.

He squinted at it between his thumb and finger.

"Good specimen," he said, "first-class specimen. You can see the stratifications with your eye."

He paused; then he went on:

"I never believed chemists could build up a diamond. Of course they build up rubies, and they do it cleverly, deuced cleverly, but you can always tell by the bubbles in them; they can't get the bubbles out."

He moved my diamond out a little farther from his eye.

"I suppose it is insufficient pressure. If they could get the angular cavities that are in corundum, they would be on the way; of course they would never get the steady glow of the genuine ruby. But they would fool the old ladies in a drawing-room."

Then his voice went into a piping note.

"You would pass for the owner of rubies if you were rich enough to back up the hypothesis."

He twisted my stone around in his fingers; then he pointed to the case under his hand, and set out a tray of diamonds.

He selected a table diamond as large as my false one and set above a platinum band. I could not have told the difference.

My diamond was worth four hundred dollars. Bartoldi said there was not a stone in the tray under five thousand dollars.

I stepped back to look at them from a little distance, about the distance one would observe a diamond on a woman's hand at dinner across the table. I could not see any difference between the two stones. They could have been interchanged, and they would have fooled me at the distance. But they didn't fool Bartoldi.

"Not much alike," he said; "your stone has a sleek look."

I did not see that. I told him I didn't see it.

I knew that aspect of artificial stones, that appearance as if they were pressed instead of cut. But it was the aspect of artificial stones of a lower order than the one I had shown to Bartoldi. This one was cut, and it looked crisp to me, very nearly as crisp as the best one. But there is where the trained eye comes in. Walker knew it was false, and Bartoldi knew it instantly. He could see the stratifications with his eye.

I could see them with a good lens, but I could not see the sleek look, and I moved toward the tray on the counter to get a close view. I did not move directly ahead; I moved to one side—and I discovered two persons who had come into the shop behind me.

I took up my diamond, and stood out of the way at once. I had no wish to delay a customer. I was only idling with a laboratory diamond, and Bartoldi had to sell jewels to keep his shop going. I could not take up his time unless he happened to be at leisure.

The two persons who had come in at once attracted my attention. They would have attracted the attention of anybody, even if there had been nothing to follow. If one had chanced to observe them, one would have stopped and considered them anywhere.

One would have been forced to think about them. They would have stimulated one's curiosity. No one could have passed those two persons without undertaking to formulate some explanation; and to me there was something more than their mere appearance.

In my mind there was a vague impression that I had seen them in some other place. I could not at the moment remember the place; it was what psychologists call subconscious, I suppose. At any rate it did not crystallize into a memory. But it remained as a sort of atmosphere behind the vivid impression they made on me.

The two persons were an old man and a girl. The two words go together, but the two persons did not go together in any sense. The girl was not past sixteen, and the man was past seventy. That would be all right, an old man and his granddaughter, you would say.

But it was not all right. That was just exactly the impression that was so cryingly conspicuous. It was not all right!

The man was very well dressed; everything about him was of the best quality, and distinguished—perhaps just a little too distinguished, a little too vivid. When one thought about it, one saw that he was dressed somewhat for a younger part. There was a bit of color, a suggestion of youth that the man did not have.

He was an old man, but he was a vigorous old man, and he had the air and manner of wealth about him. I can't precisely point out these indicatory signs, but they were easily to be marked, and they are not often successfully assumed. I suppose a clever actor could do it. Walker used to say that the best actors were not on the stage; they were in Joliet.

Now, that is what the man looked like—one of the idle rich, grown old in an atmosphere of luxury. He ought to have had, as I figured him up, a town house, a country estate, a yacht, and very nearly every vice! His eyes, his bad mouth and his fat ears were good evidential signs. I thought I knew the type!

The girl filled me with a sort of wonder. She wore a little cheap hand-me-down dress that must have come from a village shop, and it looked as though she had slept in it. She had slept in it!

The sort of crumpled-up appearance of that cheap material could not be mistaken. She wore a straw hat lined with vivid color and loaded with soiled artificial flowers. Her shoes were run down a bit. She was generally soiled, as she would have been if she had traveled in a day coach and slept in her clothes—and that is precisely what she had done.

But all this could not obscure the fact that she was pretty, in a sort of way. She had a pliant figure, and the charms that go along with youth. Sleeping in one's clothes, and the grime of a journey can't obscure that. She was young, and she had what youth has.

Now you understand why I said that the two together puzzled me. Either alone would not attract a glance, and certainly not a line of speculation. But the two together, as I have insisted, called upon you for an explanation.

They puzzled me but they did not puzzle Bartoldi. I suppose he understood it quicker than I. I understood it pretty quickly, just as you have, no doubt, understood it all along, and as Bartoldi understood it at a glance.

They came up to the glass counter, and the man asked to see a diamond ring.

The girl did not look up. She did not say anything. She seemed to wish to get as far as possible under the soiled hat.

Bartoldi set out some trays beside the one already on the table. The old man moved a little to one side and the girl came quite close to the glass counter. She bent her head down over the stones as though she wished to see the rings and at the same time keep under cover of the soiled hat.

She did not say a word. But she knew precisely what she wanted, for she suddenly put out her hand and picked up the table diamond that had lain beside my artificial stone on the glass case. She slipped the stone on her finger and stepped back as though to be hidden a little by the old man.

I got a surprise.

"Gad," I said to myself, "big wages! Will he stand for it?"

Well, he did stand for it. He was a royal old sport; I will say that for him.

Bartoldi said the price was five thousand dollars, and the old boy never turned an eyelash. He made a careless gesture. I don't think he even O.K.'d the thing with a word.

He took a flat leather case out of his pocket, got out a draft, asked Bartoldi for a pen, or rather indicated the wish for a pen with a fiddling of his fingers, and when he got it, indorsed the draft. Then he showed Bartoldi a letter that was in the envelope that had contained the draft.

I followed them to the door. There was a taxicab waiting; they got in and went up the Avenue.

That type of man ought to have a house somewhere on the Avenue; it was August; the house would be closed; I began to put things together.

I was standing there when Walker came up. I hailed him.

"Walker," I said, "you got here a moment too late. You see that taxi-cab?"

He made a little whimsical gesture.

"I see everything," he said, "that the devil puts out to annoy me; what's in the taxicab?"

"There's a case in it," I said, "for the District Court of the United States, on the criminal side, or I'm a poor detective."

"All detectives are poor," said Walker. "If they were rich, they would have a town house, a country place and a string of hunters."

"Well," I said, "that's what the old boy in the taxicab has got; and he's got something else that the United States doesn't allow him to take across a state line."

Walker looked at me queerly. He put the tip of his finger to his forehead.

"Touch of the heat?"

"Look here," I said, "isn't this sort of thing just as much in your line of duty as trying to prevent the crooked cashier from boring from within? Isn't the United States by a fairly recent statute, helping virtue to evade the dragon?"

Walker's face wrinkled into a twisted smile.

"It's helping the clever *fille de joie* to levy a little blackmail on the side."

"Wrong dope, in this instance," I said.

I began to describe to him the incident and the two persons. I described them carefully, minutely, and he listened without a word and without a motion. He stood perfectly still, there in the hot street before Bartoldi's mammoth shop.

But his manner had changed. He had now, I noted from the very impassive aspect of the man, a deep, a profound, a moving interest in this affair. He cursed softly as though he chopped the words with his teeth.

"Ten minutes too late!" he said. "Where did they go?"

Walker was motionless for a moment, his head down, his eyes narrowed in a profound reflection.

I interrupted him with a repetition of his words.

"Ten minutes too late!" I said. "You are two minutes too late. The taxicab has hardly disappeared in the traffic yonder."

I pointed up the Avenue. Walker did not look up.

"I was thinking of Bartoldi," he said. "I am ten minutes too late for Bartoldi."

"That's right," I said. "Bartoldi could have told you who this man was. He must have known him."

"Oh, no," said Walker. "Bartoldi didn't know him."

I was astonished.

"Surely Bartoldi knew him," I said.

Walker's voice became a sort of drawl.

"Surely he did not know him. Bartoldi would not have been a party to this man's criminal adventures."

I laughed.

"What does Bartoldi care about criminal adventures? He's a dealer in jewels."

"He will care about this criminal adventure," said Walker.

Then he looked suddenly at me.

"Where do you think they went?"

I told him what I thought. This type of person would have a house on the Avenue; it would be closed in August.

Walker shook his head.

"I think I know where they have gone," he said.

Again I looked at him in astonishment.

"Then you know who this man is?"

Walker replied with an abrupt query:

"Did you see the inside of his hand—the right hand? That was the thing to see."

"How about the girl?" I replied, for Walker's indirections were putting me on my mettle. "Her hand will be the thing to see; it's got Bartoldi's diamond on it."

He looked up rather vaguely.

"I am puzzled about the girl; I do not understand what the girl has to do with it."

I laughed.

"Bartoldi understood," I said.

"Bartoldi!"

Walker seemed to bounce out of his reflection.

"The devil! We've got to get back his diamond."

He darted suddenly out to the traffic of the Avenue, hailed a taxicab and beckoned me to get in with him.

I got in and we went up Fifth Avenue. We were held in a jam of vehicles a block or two farther on.

"And so," I said, "you think the girl is a nice little country cousin, an esteemed relative—esteemed to the tune of a five-thousand-dollar diamond?"

Walker was fingering his face in reflection.

"Nonsense!" he said. "The girl's no relation to him."

"Then why the five-thousand-dollar diamond?"

"That's what I would like to know," said Walker.

I laughed. The thing was too absurd.

"If the wage of a sin is a five-thousand-dollar diamond, there's got to be the sin to earn it. That old sport was not taking any chance on getting the value of his money."

"O. K.," said Walker.

"Then you think he has been paid for it?" I said.

"Surely," said Walker, "that man has been paid for it."

The taxicab turned out of the Avenue presently when the jam of vehicles was released, and stopped before the Grand Central Station.

Walker paused a moment when we got down.

"If I put the thing together correctly," he said, "they will be here. The girl came in for her diamond.... How she earned it puzzles me.... The man had to get through with it as quickly as he could."

He made a little gesture.

"From the station to Bartoldi's in a taxicab and back to the first train out—that would be his plan—to hurry."

He added: "It was a risk, a big risk. But he had to take it. He couldn't trust anybody; he had to do it himself."

I looked at Walker with what I imagined was an ironical smile.

"Then he would not be guilty under the statute," I said, "for he only brought the little baggage in to buy her a diamond."

Walker seemed in a sort of reflection.

"Oh, yes," he said, "he is guilty."

"Then you want him?" I asked.

Walker suddenly looked at me with his eyes wide.

"Surely," he said.

"Then why don't you hurry?" I demanded.

He looked at me with a leisurely interest.

"If he's here," he said, "he can't get out. I've got three of the best agents of the Department in there—sent them up when I started to Bartoldi's to meet you."

"But how would they know him?" I asked.

"They would know him by a scar in his hand," replied Walker.

"They ought to know him by a girl on his arm," I said.

Walker's voice became reflective.

"I wonder if she could be his granddaughter, after all!"

I laughed. That laugh was like the key to a memory. I at once remembered where I had seen this man and the girl.

It was at the end of the path that follows the sea south at Bar Harbor. There is a great house where the path ends. It was closed; the shutters were up, and the grounds only casually kept; I remembered it now. I had undertaken one afternoon to get through from this sea-path to the village street, and had wandered into an immense sunken garden. I was making no sound.

The grass and leaves had covered the paths; it was very still, and presently I heard the murmur of voices. I wondered who could be here, for as I have said, the place was closed, and I was discovering that there was no way through to the village street. I went forward a few steps, and beyond me, standing in an angle of the garden, obscured by an immense flowering vine, were this old man and this girl.

I remembered the scene perfectly, now that I had the key to it.

The old man was speaking in a low voice, as though he urged something, offered something, and the girl was listening in the attitude in which I had observed her this afternoon, her head down, her arms hanging. I had gone out quietly; I remember the explanation that presented itself. The old man must be the owner of the place, and the girl a keeper's daughter, perhaps. The memory bore out my impression, the impression which I received to-day and the impression which had evidently convinced Bartoldi.

I told it all to Walker, very carefully and in detail, as we went into the great lobby and down to the train exits. Walker caught my arm in his big hand.

"That explains it," he commented.

Then he stopped abruptly.

"By the way," he said, as though it had just occurred to him and he had now leisure to think about it, "let me have a look at that artificial diamond."

I took the piece of tissue paper out of my waistcoat pocket and handed it to him. He unfolded the paper, took the diamond out and retained it in his hand. We crossed through the throngs of people everywhere grouped about in the great station, to the exit indicating the evening train to Bar Harbor. We entered the little group, and I realized suddenly that we were close behind the old man and the girl. They were facing toward the gate.

Suddenly Walker opened his hand and dropped my diamond to the floor. It clattered at the feet of the girl, and Walker stooped swiftly and picked it up.

"Your daughter," he said, speaking to the old man, "has dropped the setting out of her ring; permit me to return it."

The man turned instantly like a trapped animal. For a moment both of his hands went into the pockets of his coat, and for an instant his face was uncertain, vague, deadly; then he put out his hand for the diamond.

Walker gave it to him and turned to me.

"Perhaps," he said, "we had better see if the trunks got on. We have nearly ten minutes to wait."

And he walked away toward the great stair leading to the baggage room.

The girl did not move; she did not speak; she remained as she had stood in Bartoldi's shop, her head down, concealed as far as she was able to conceal it, under the drooping hat loaded with soiled roses. Walker was crossing toward the great stair in his long stride and I hurrying in my astonishment to overtake him.

"The devil, man!" I cried when I came up. "Why did you give him my diamond?"

"I wanted to see if there was a scar in his hand," said Walker. "He had it."

"Then you know him?"

"Surely," said Walker.

"Aren't you going to arrest him?"

Walker had returned to his careless manner.

"No," he said, "I am not going to arrest him. You saw his hands go into his pockets. There would have been a lot of people killed if it hadn't been for your diamond. It's lucky I thought of it; besides, I had to see the inside of his hand."

"But my diamond," I said, "when will I get it?"

Walker continued in his leisurely drawl:

"You will get your diamond when Bartoldi gets his."

"When will that be?" I insisted.

"Right now," replied Walker.

Then he paused in his stride, took off his hat and extended it for a moment above his head like a tired person who would relax from the fatigue of travel.

Immediately three persons, two men and a woman between them, carrying bags, coats and the usual articles of travel, came out from the crowd pouring into the station from the street and crossed hurriedly into the group waiting at the entrance for the Bar Harbor train.

Then a dramatic thing happened.

I could see the old man clearly; he was watching Walker out of the tail of his eye, and he kept his hands in his pockets, but he was not watching the three persons who came into the group as though seeking the train for which he was bound; and as they passed, quicker than the eye, the man's hands were seized, dragged out of his pockets and snapped into handcuffs. The pistols gripped in his hands were swept out; they fell to the floor.

"The devil!" I cried. "The old boy is the most dangerous Lothario I ever saw."

Walker replied in his leisurely drawl:

"He's the most dangerous bank swindler you ever saw."

* * * *

The girl had been questioned, and the thing was now clear. Walker explained it all on the way to Bartoldi's in a taxicab. I had my diamond in my pocket, and Walker had Bartoldi's to exchange for the forged draft. The old man was Vronsky, the most notorious forger in the world. He had bribed this girl, the janitress of the Empire Bank at Bar Harbor, to steal a book of blank drafts and some sheets of stationery. It was easy to do; the book of blanks was lying on the bookkeeper's desk in the package as it had come from the printer, and the stationery had never been locked up.

With the blanks bearing the secret water mark of the bank, Vronsky was able to forge drafts on New York and place them, establishing his identity by a letter from the bank officials on this stationery, in which they said they were sending him the draft which he intended to pay out, and giving its amount and number.

"It was a clever scheme," Walker added. "The secret water mark on the draft blanks would show that they were genuine—that's what convinced Bartoldi; and the forged letter would show the identity of the man who undertook to place it. The forgery gave Vronsky no trouble; the problem was how to get the blanks and letter paper."

"And he got them with a diamond," I said.

Walker's drawl lengthened.

"Precisely as we got him."

And so this adventure opened with a diamond and closed with the arrest of one of the worst criminals in the world. What was it I wrote in the opening paragraph of this case? Go back and read it.

CHAPTER VIII

THE EXPERT DETECTIVE

Walker kept two dog-eared magazines in a pigeonhole of his desk, with a story marked in each. He kept them, he said, to reduce enthusiasm, as a doctor keeps a drug to reduce a fever. They were handed, with the regularity of a habit, to two types of visitors who annoyed him: those persons who volubly admired the professional detective; and that other class who assured him that the inspired amateur, as, for example, some local prosecutor in a criminal case, could outwit the acutest counselors of darkness.

I include the two stories in their instructive order.

* * * *

The State had completed its case.

The conviction of the prisoners seemed beyond question.

Incident by incident, the expert detective, Barkman, had coupled up the circumstantial evidence until it seemed to link the prisoners inevitably to the crime. He was a big man, with eyes blue like a piece of crockery, a wide face and a cruel, irregular jaw. One felt that no sentiment restrained him; that he would carry out any undertaking to its desperate end.

He sat now in the witness chair. He was the last witness for the State, and, now that the case was complete, he had been turned over for cross-examination.

It was afternoon. A sheet of sunlight entering through open windows lay on the court room. It was a court room of a little city in the South; a city but newly awakened to industrial activities, and the conduct of its administration of justice still adhered to older and more deliberate forms.

The court room was crowded with people down to the very railing that separated the attorneys' tables from the crowd.

The judge, a tall man, with a long, mild, unhealthy face, sat on the bench. To the right of him and a step below was the clerk. The jury were in chairs along the wall to the left of the bench. And between the bench and jurors sat the witness.

The prosecuting attorney was before his table, a little to the right of the first step to the bench. There were law books on his table, and two polka-dot handkerchiefs lying loosely on some papers. The man was no longer concerned with these articles. He sat back from the table, his fingers linked together, his face lifted as in some reflection.

Farther to the right, in two chairs against the railing, were the prisoners. One, a big old man with a splotched, dissipated face and his hair cropped close to his skull. Folds of fat lay along the base of his neck, partly concealed by a white silk handkerchief held in place under his chin by a long old-fashioned garnet pin. His companion was a little, thin, fox-faced man who moved nervously in his chair.

The most striking figure in the court room was the attorney for the prisoners.

He sat between them, a chair's width in advance, before his table. There was nothing whatever on this table except an ink pot, two pens and a big blotting sheet. There was also a thick pad of foolscap paper provided for the convenience of the attorney in taking any note of the testimony, but there was no word written on it.

The lawyer was a huge bulk of a man. He sat relaxed in his chair. His thick, black hair was brushed smoothly. It was of an oily, glossy blackness. His big, thick features were putty-colored, as though the man's skin had no vitality. His eyes were very nearly closed; his mouth sagged open, the thick lips holding a cigar that was not lighted.

Every detail of his dress was immaculate and arranged with extreme care.

The man was perhaps sixty, but, in the big relaxed body and heavy face, age was indefinite. He now took the cigar out of his mouth and laid it down on the table. He moved like one coming out of a dream.

He had not immediately taken charge of the witness when the prosecutor had released him for examination. But now, finally, at the judge's words, "Proceed, Colonel," he at last looked up.

"You are an expert detective, Mr. Barkman."

The voice had a strange dwindling whine as though it came from some cavernous depth in the man's immense body.

The witness looked about with a vague smile. "Well, Colonel," he said, "I have had some experience."

"You have had a great deal of experience. You were Chief of Police, then you set up a detective agency. You have had a lot of experience in criminal investigation. And you have usually been right."

This was generous treatment when the reverse was indicated.

The detective was not conspicuous for the confidence of the community in a profession too often subject to cloud. His employment in the bank affairs had followed from his intimate association with Halloway, an association, as all knew, resulting from the handling of a questionable matter in the banker's private life.

The bank did not require a retained detective.

Was this man's sinecure gratitude in the banker, or a sort of blackmail? Here was material with which a reflection on the witness could have been assembled. But the attorney chose rather to admit the man's superior mental acumen in criminal affairs.

The witness moved in his chair. "Well, Colonel," he said, "I try to be right."

"And you have nearly always been right," continued the attorney. "In the Deal case you maintained that the decedent had not been killed by a bullet fired from a cellar grating at a hundred yards along the street east of the man's window, and it was afterward shown that the trajectory of a bullet fired from that point would have crashed into an electric light midway of the distance. And in the Littlewood case, you said the evidences of a struggle were manufactured, because the slant of wood fibers in the broken window sash showed that the pressure had been exerted from within the room and not from without."

The voice ascended into a lighter drawl with a facetious note in it.

"You have had a lot of experience, and you have had a lot of work, but you have not got rich at it. You would like to be rich, wouldn't you?"

The witness laughed. "I suppose everybody would like to be rich, Colonel."

The attorney smiled, a big, loose, vacuous sort of smile.

"Old Bill," he said, "here behind me, and Lyin' Louie would like to be rich, but they are more likely to be hanged." He laughed again. "You are not afraid of being hanged, Mr. Barkman?"

Everybody laughed. The eccentricities of this attorney were one of the attractions of the court room. They were good-naturedly overlooked by the officers of the court, who had been associated with the man for a lifetime in an old-fashioned civilization, leisurely and considerate.

The attorney made a gesture as of one putting by a pleasantry of the moment.

"This was a very ingeniously constructed crime?"

The witness was now in an excellent humor. "I'd say it was, Colonel," he replied. "It was slick enough to fool me."

"Ah!" The attorney continued. "I had forgotten that. It was your theory in the beginning that the president of the Trader's Bank, Mr. Halloway, had accomplished the robbery himself, and, afterward, dropped dead in his own house. He lay on the floor, when the body was discovered, by the side of the library table. It was thought that in falling his head had struck the heavy carved foot of the table, causing the injury to the skull that resulted in death. The physicians first called in were inclined to agree with that theory. The immense strain of a criminal adventure might have caused the accident after the man had returned to his house. Emotional cataclysms have been known to bring on attacks of acute indigestion or the rupture of a defective heart."

"Sure, Colonel," the witness assented, "that's what the thing looked like; and I was fooled about it; I admit it. There was no evidence of a struggle in the room. It was only after Doctor North said the man had been killed by a blow, probably with the poker, that I got onto the right track."

The attorney made a drawling assent.

"Yes," he said, "that was a bad find."

His voice went again into a strange laugh.

"It was mighty near a hangin' find for Old Bill and Lyin' Louie! You got on better then, Mr. Barkman. You found two polka-dot handkerchiefs that had been stuffed down into a vase in the library, and then you found Old Bill and Lyin' Louie. Now you are goin' to hang 'em, I reckon."

There was a suppressed giggle in the court room. It was not shared by the prisoners.

The big, old man of the close-cropped skull plucked the attorney by the sleeve and spoke in an audible whisper.

"Looka here, Colonel," he said, "I thought you was defendin' us."

The attorney replied, a higher note in his deep drawl.

"Yes," he said, "that's what I am doing. But you've got no sense, Bill! You never had any sense. If you had had any sense you would not have been in the pen-i-ten-tia-ry house. There was no reason for you going to the pen-i-ten-tia-ry. Old Lansky tried to make a bank-cracker out of you—I was in the cell with him on the night he was hanged—he said you had no sense. He said you would never make anything but a fence, and a damned poor fence ... that's what he said, Bill."

He interrupted the long narrative by getting ponderously on his feet. He reached out and took the two handkerchiefs from the table of the prosecuting attorney and laid them down on his own.

Then he addressed the witness.

"Now, Mr. Barkman," he said, "I'd like you to tell us precisely what you think happened on the night of the twenty-seventh. I want you to reconstruct this crime for us. I want you to show us just how Old Bill and Lyin' Louie went about this thing."

The witness moved as though rearranging himself in his chair. He shifted his shoulder a little to one side and he looked around toward the jury.

"Well, Colonel," he said, "I think I can tell you just exactly what happened."

He was not expecting to be interrupted. But he was interrupted by a sort of explosive assent.

The big attorney was looking at him, resting his huge body on both hands, on the table. The witness was for a moment disconcerted, then he went on:

"It was like this," he said, "as I figure it out. Everybody knows that Old Bill was a bank-cracker."

Again there was a sort of booming interruption.

"He was never a good bank-cracker," the lawyer exploded; "he was a poor bank-cracker. He was such a damn poor bank-cracker that he got into the pen-i-ten-tia-ry house!"

The witness laughed.

"Anyway, Colonel," he said, "when Louie drifted in here, the two of them fixed up this game and they carried it out slick."

Again the lawyer introduced an interruption.

"Now, that is just what I am anxious to know, Mr. Barkman. I am anxious to know precisely what they did and how they did it. I want to know, in detail, everything that happened that night."

"Well," replied the witness, "this is the way I figure it out, Colonel, and I think it's straight dope: these men fixed up their plan and Louie hung around until he found that the bank president was alone in his house. That was the night his family went to the Springs. It was in the newspapers. Everybody knew it. Then about midnight they went up to Mr. Halloway's house."

"And how did they get into the house?" inquired the lawyer.

"That was no trouble," said the witness. "They rang the bell. They wanted Mr. Halloway to come down just as he did come down, with his dressing gown on, like he was found dead in the library."

The attorney had changed his posture. He was idly fingering the two polka-dot handkerchiefs.

The witness went on:

"When Mr. Halloway opened the door, one of these crooks jammed a pistol against him. They shut the door and marched him into the library. And there they told him what they were going to do. They held him up, right there in the library, and forced him to give them the combination to the bank safe."

"And how were they to know," inquired the attorney, "that the combination which the banker gave them was the correct one? Would not his impulse be—would not any one's impulse be—to give an incorrect combination of figures?"

The witness laughed.

"Old Bill would know the trick," he said. "They would ask the banker to give the combination. They would write it down as he gave it; then they would wait a little while and ask him again, and if he had made it up, he would not be able to remember. That's an old trick. It was done in the North Hampton bank robbery, where they burned the cashier's feet for lying."

The big attorney swung around toward his clients.

"Did you ever hear of that, Bill?"

"No," said the prisoner, "I never did."

Again the attorney laughed that vague, futile laugh.

"I believe you, Bill," he said, "although nobody else does—I'm paid to believe you."

He turned back to the witness.

"What happened then?"

The big prisoner with the folded white handkerchief for a cravat was mumbling incoherently.

The attorney paid no attention.

He looked at the witness. "Go on, Mr. Barkman," he said. "What did they do next?"

"Well," said the witness, "when they had got the correct combination written down, they put a gun against Mr. Halloway and made him go over to the telephone. They made him call up the watchman at the bank and tell him just what he has sworn here Mr. Halloway told him that night: that his child was sick and the doctor wanted him to come right home. Mr. Halloway had to say just what they told him to say, because there they stood with a gun against him. They could hear every word he said. The bank watchman asked him what he could do about leaving the bank, and they made Mr. Halloway say to him over the telephone, to go ahead out to his house at once and that he himself would drive over in his car and stay in the bank until the watchman got back; then they hung up the receiver."

The lawyer put a query:

"How do you suppose they were standing while Mr. Halloway was calling the bank?"

The witness got up.

"Mr. Halloway was of course facing the telephone and the man with the gun was standing behind him with the muzzle jammed against his back. That would be the way they would be standing."

He was about to sit down, but the lawyer interrupted him:

"Just a minute."

He turned to the prisoner sitting on his left.

"Louie," he said, "I want you to go over to Mr. Barkman and show us just how you were holding that pistol against the banker's back while he was talking over the telephone. We'll say Mr. Barkman's the banker."

Everybody in the court room was astonished at this slip of the attorney. It would appear that he, like every one else, was convinced of the guilt of the prisoners, and that this conviction had thus unconsciously appeared in his words.

The man seemed not to realize what he had said. But the prisoner saw it at once.

"Colonel," he objected, "how can I show him how it was done when I didn't do it?"

The attorney made an exasperated gesture.

"Oh, Louie," he said, "you are such a liar that nobody believes anything you say. Do what I tell you."

Then he stooped over the prisoner.

"Just a moment, Judge," he explained; "I have got to encourage my client."

He whispered something in the man's ear.

The prisoner rose and went over to the witness; he took him by the shoulders and turned him around toward the judge, so that his back was to the jury. He moved him until he got him in precisely the position which he wished and then he thrust his long forefinger in the man's back, with the other fingers doubled up.

"How's that, Colonel?" he said.

"Well," said the attorney, "what do you think about it, Louie? Do you think it's O.K.?"

"Sure," said the prisoner.

Then he came back and sat down in the chair.

The whole court room was amused and astonished. It was as good as a theater.

The attorney returned to his examination of the witness.

"Proceed, Mr. Barkman," he said. "What did they do next? Did they make Mr. Halloway go over to the bank? His car was seen there and he was, himself, seen going in, by some persons passing at the end of the street. He was alone. How did they make him go over there alone, accomplish the robbery, and come back to his house?"

Again the witness smiled shrewdly.

"They didn't make him do it," he said. "Old Bill there, he's about the size of Mr. Halloway."

He turned about to the jurors.

"Mr. Halloway was a man, as you all know, about as big as I am. Old Bill put on the banker's hat and his long light overcoat. The runabout stood under the porte-cochère outside. He went out, got in this car and drove it over to the bank. He had the banker's key to the door and he had the combination to the safe, so he went in, opened the safe, picked out the money and brought it back with him."

The attorney suddenly interrupted.

"Now, there," he said, "right there. Why did they take only big bills and not smaller currency? There were twenty thousand dollars taken in big bills—five-hundred and one-thousand-dollar bills. Why did they take that and not the smaller currency?"

"I can explain that," said the witness. "You see they had to hide this money after they got it—they had to look out for that; they might have to move pretty quickly. They could not trust anybody to keep it for them and they were afraid to conceal it, so they would have to carry it around with them. That's the reason they took big bills."

"Ah," said the attorney, "I understand it now. It puzzled me a lot. I could not see what they meant by taking big bills and leaving the rest of the money; but it's clear now."

He swung suddenly around to the prisoners. "Louie," he said, "you never told me that."

The creature grinned, his face broken into a queer extended smile.

But the big prisoner to the right showed evidence of no such conciliatory mood.

He got up.

"Judge," he said, "we're bein' double crossed. I paid the Colonel, here, a hundred dollars in honest money to defend us, and just look what he's doin' to us."

Everybody laughed.

The lawyer turned about and spoke to the man as he might have spoken to an impertinent child.

"Sit down, Bill," he said. "Louie knows that I am making a proper defense, don't you, Louie?"

The little fox-faced man continued to grin. But he said nothing.

"Now, Bill," the lawyer went on gently as to a child, "Louie's got some sense; not much. He learned how to open registered envelopes, when he started in to be a mail clerk, by watching the post-office inspectors rolling a pen handle under the flap; and he learned to feel for money in the envelope before he opened it. The post-office inspectors taught him that. Louie had sense enough to learn it. He learned it well. He can tell the feel of a bill through the thickest envelope that was ever mailed. But you are a fool, Bill; Lansky told me that. Nobody but a fool, after he robbed the Norristown bank, would have hidden the money in the loft of an abandoned schoolhouse, with a trail of cinders leading from the window up to the trap in the ceiling. Anybody but a fool would have wiped his feet off before he climbed in the window."

The whole court room was convulsed with laughter; even the judge smiled.

Nothing could have been more of the essence of comedy than these passages between the attorney and his client.

The big lawyer turned again to the witness. "Now, Mr. Barkman," he said, "what did they do when Bill got back with the money?"

"They finished the job," replied the witness.

"Well," said the attorney, "what did they do?"

"It is clear what they did," replied the detective; "they killed Mr. Halloway with the fire poker, then they hid the two handkerchiefs they had over their faces when they came in, and then they got out of town."

The witness sat back in his chair as though he had finished with his testimony.

The big attorney stood up. The whole aspect of the man, as by the snap of a switch, had undergone a transformation. The huge bulk of him was vital. His heavy slack face was firm.

"Mr. Barkman," he said, "why did the men who killed Hiram Halloway wear no masks on their faces?"

"They did wear masks on their faces—they're on the table before you."

The lawyer did not look down at the articles before him. His voice was now hard and accurate like the point of a steel tool.

"Take it as a hypothetical question then. Suppose they wore no masks. What would that fact indicate?"

The attorney for the State rose.

"I object," he said. "There must be evidence in the case tending to support the assumed facts in a hypothetical question."

"The evidence shall be presently indicated," replied the lawyer.

The judge passed on the objection at once.

"The Colonel promises to point out the evidence later. He may go on; the witness has been introduced as an expert."

The lawyer again faced the man in the chair. He repeated his question.

The witness seemed doubtful.

"I don't know," he said.

"You don't know! Reflect, Mr. Barkman. Would it not mean that the person or persons who accomplished this criminal act felt that they were so well known to Hiram Halloway that no ordinary disguise could conceal their identity?"

The witness did not immediately reply, and the lawyer went on:

"And is not this the reason why Hiram Halloway was killed?"

"Why he was killed!" repeated the man in the chair.

"Yes, precisely the reason. One must credit even a common thief with some intelligence. No one uselessly adds the crime of murder to a lesser crime. Masked assassins wholly unknown to the decedent would have gagged and bound him. It would have answered their purpose as well. But not the purpose of a known, unmasked assassin. Safety for him lay only in the banker's death."

The attorney added:

"That death was so unavoidably necessary—to cover the identity of the assassin—that the evidences of an accidental death were arranged with elaborate care. Is it not true?"

The witness had been twisting his feet about; his face uncertain. Now it took on a dogged look.

"It's true that the thing was a slick job."

The attorney took one step toward the witness. "Now, Mr. Barkman," he said, "can you tell me why assassins who had so carefully staged this tragedy to appear accidental should leave behind them two handkerchiefs, with eye-holes cut in them, thrust carelessly into a vase on a table? They might be found, and that discovery would, at once, negative the theory of accidental death."

"They wanted to get rid of the masks."

"But if they wore no masks? Is it not inconceivable that they would have placed them there to jeopardize all that they had so carefully planned?"

The witness was watching the attorney, the dogged look deepening in his face.

"If they didn't wear masks, of course they wouldn't have put them there—it would have been a fool thing."

The attorney moved out closer to the witness. The point, as one might say, of his voice seemed to sharpen.

"Now, Mr. Barkman, if these masks were not put into the vase on the table by the assassins, then they were put there by somebody else; and if they were not put there on the night of the robbery, they were put there later; and if they were put there by some one later, it was one who had access to the house later; and if they were put there by one having access to the house after it was established the banker did not die from a natural cause, then they were put there to deceive."

He paused, and his final sentence descended like a hammer:

"And the deception in presenting false evidence of *two* men would consist in the fact that but *one* man had, in fact, accomplished the crime."

The prosecuting attorney was on his feet.

"Your honor," he said, "this is all built up on the theory that the assassins did not wear masks. There is no evidence to support such a theory. The handkerchiefs that the assassins took off of their faces and hid in the vase are here in the case for everybody to see."

The attorney for the prisoners put out his hand and took up the two polka-dot handkerchiefs which were lying on the table before him.

"It is the cleverest criminal," he said, "who always makes the most striking blunder. The accomplished assassin of Lord William Russell carried away the knife with which his victim was supposed to have cut his own throat. When the human intelligence, set on murder, undertakes to falsify the order of events, the absurdity of its error increases with its cunning."

He shook the two handkerchiefs out and stretched them in his fingers.

"They are here for everybody to see," he echoed, "and if everybody will look, he will see that these two handkerchiefs were never tied around the faces of assassins; he will see—everybody—that, while these handkerchiefs have eye-holes cut in them, the corners of them are as smooth and uncreased as though they had been ironed; if they had been tied around the faces of assassins, they would show the strain and the fold of the knot!"

He turned now toward the judge.

"Your Honor," he said, "the elaborate ingenuity of this whole criminal plan is utterly beyond the feeble intelligence of these prisoners. It is the work of some competent person; some person well known to the decedent; some person who knew a disguise to be useless; some one who had access to the house and was able to set up the evidence of a second theory after the first had failed—such an one was the assassin of Hiram Halloway."

There was absolute silence in the court room. The witness sat gripping the arms of his chair, his face distended as with some physical pressure.

The big attorney, at the end of his significant pause, added a final sentence:

"And now, that we have found the money, we can name the man!"

The prosecuting attorney, utterly astonished, put the question, the answer to which the whole court room awaited:

"Found the money! Where?"

The big lawyer sat down in his chair; his huge body relaxed; his face assumed its vague placidity and his voice descended into its old, deep-seated, dwindling whine:

"It's sewed up in the lining of Mr. Barkman's coat. Lyin' Louie felt it when he posed him for the jury."

CHAPTER IX

THE "MYSTERIOUS STRANGER" DEFENSE

"Now, Ellen," said the attorney, "I want you to tell us precisely why you called to me when you ran out of the house—why you said, 'Save me, Colonel.'"

"I was scared," replied the witness. "I didn't know what was going to happen to me."

"You thought the same thing that had happened to the lawyer, Mr. Collander, might also happen to you."

"I don't know, Colonel. I was scared."

It was the third day of the criminal trial. Colonel Armant had put the prisoner on the stand in her own defense. It seemed a desperate hazard. A woman remains an experiment as a witness. The old experts about the court room were pretty nearly a unit against the experiment in this case. The prisoner was too much of an enigma; one of those little, faded, blonde women, with a placid, inscrutable face—capable of everything or of nothing, as one chose to assume it.

The big attorney went on.

"You did know that something had happened to Mr. Collander?"

"I heard the shots—yes, I knew something had happened to him."

"Just a moment, on this feature," continued the attorney. "You do not agree with the chief of police about the number of shots fired; you thought there were three shots; one, and then two together, or almost together?"

The prosecuting attorney interrupted.

"If you are going to lead the witness, Colonel," he said, "why don't you lead her to some purpose? Why don't you lead her to say there was only *one* shot?"

The huge counsel for the prisoner put out his hand toward the speaker, in the gesture of one who brushes aside a disturbing fly, but he did not otherwise move in his chair. His whole body was in repose. He spoke without moving a muscle.

"Now, Ellen," he said, "the prosecuting attorney makes it a point against you that you were expecting something to happen. What do you say about that? You don't deny it, do you?"

"Well, Colonel," replied the witness, "I thought something might happen to Mr. Collander. I thought it all along."

"Then you did expect it?"

"Yes," replied the witness, "I suppose you could say I did expect it."

The attorney rose.

"That brings us to another point made against you."

He took up a weapon lying on the table before him. It was a thirty-two-caliber cylinder revolver of the usual type.

"You can identify this weapon?" the attorney asked.

"It is the revolver that Mr. Collander kept in his bedroom."

"Now, Ellen," said the attorney, "the State has introduced testimony to show that you took this pistol to the gunsmith, Mr. Parks, and had him clean it and load it for you. That was on Tuesday, a week before Mr. Collander's death. The prosecuting attorney calls on me to explain that incident on some theory, if I can, which will be inconsistent with his theory that you thereby provided yourself with a weapon in order to kill Mr. Collander." He paused. "We are not concerned with anybody's theory, Ellen, but what is the truth about it?"

"I was afraid, Colonel, just as I have said. I thought there ought to be a pistol in the house that would shoot."

The attorney paused a moment as in reflection; then he went on.

"That's the second point the State makes against you. There is still another; let us get them all together so we can tell the jury precisely what they mean. The prosecuting attorney has shown, here, by a number of witnesses, that you sometimes threatened the lawyer, Mr. Collander; that you have been known to quarrel with him, and that you have more than once said you would kill him. Now, isn't that true?"

The witness hesitated a moment. She looked vaguely about the court room; presently her eyes rested on the floor.

"Yes," she said, "it's all true; but I was not the only person who wanted to kill him." She hesitated. "What I said was talk—just talk; the other people who wanted to kill him meant it."

The big attorney lifted his body with a little gesture.

"The fact is, Ellen, that you were always fond of him."

The witness continued to look down at the floor.

"Yes," she said, "too fond of him, Colonel."

The attorney seemed to draw his big body together. He stood up before his table.

"Now," he went on, "let us get all the bad features of this case together. You say other persons wished this man's death. What makes you say that, Ellen?"

"Well, Colonel," replied the witness, "that's pretty hard for me to answer. Everybody knows that Mr. Collander had a lot of enemies, a lot of people didn't like him; a lot of people who had just as much reason to threaten to kill him as I had, and they must have meant it when I didn't mean it."

"Ellen," said the attorney, "let us try to be a little more precise about this. You say that there were persons who wished to kill the lawyer, Collander; that you thought he was in danger, and that you had this weapon cleaned and loaded so he would have some means of defending himself."

The prosecuting attorney interrupted.

"Just a moment, Colonel," he said. "The witness hasn't said anything of the sort."

The attorney made an irrelevant gesture.

"Perhaps not entirely in those words," he said, "but it is the substance and intent of the answers. I shall permit her to reply for herself. What do you say about that, Ellen?"

The witness answered at once.

"That's it," she said, "that's exactly it. I thought Mr. Collander was in danger of being killed, and I thought he ought to have a pistol that was loaded and would shoot. That's why I took it to Mr. Parks."

The big attorney nodded in assent.

"Now, what made you think that the decedent was in danger of his life? You must have had some reason for it?"

"Well," said the witness, "people were always coming to see Mr. Collander. I have often heard him in a quarrel with people who came in to see him. His study opens out on the porch; they sometimes came to the porch and knocked on the door."

"They didn't always knock on the door, did they?" inquired the attorney. "Sometimes they called him?"

The witness looked at the lawyer as though she did not precisely follow his question.

"Yes," she said, "sometimes they called him."

"And then they would be standing down on the ground," continued the attorney. "The porch before the door is narrow; that would put them below Mr. Collander if he were standing in the door."

"Yes, sir," said the witness, "the ground is lower than the porch; anybody standing on the ground would be below Mr. Collander."

Again the prosecuting attorney interrupted.

"What's that go to do with it?" he said. "Are you going to drag in the 'mysterious stranger' defense?"

The big lawyer swung around on his feet.

"Your Honor," he said, addressing the judge, "I object to this expression. It is an unfair expression. It has no place in a judicial trial of which the sole object is to arrive at the truth. The prosecuting attorney has no right to undertake to prejudice the prisoner before the jury. That is an ungenerous expression. If the prisoner did not kill Mr. Collander, some one else did kill him, and if we don't know, precisely, who that other person was we cannot dismiss him as mythical, as a 'mysterious stranger,' as though he were a figment of the imagination."

The judge did not reply. He was accustomed to these passages between the attorneys, staged always for effect, and he took no part in them if he could avoid it.

The prosecuting attorney replied with ill-concealed irony.

"If the prisoner did not kill him!" he echoed.

"Quite so," replied the Colonel, "and for your benefit, sir, I will say that I propose to show, in a moment, that she not only did not kill him, but that she could not have killed him."

The prosecuting attorney made a vague gesture in the air with his extended fingers. The aspect of irony remained.

"Go to it," he said.

"Now, Ellen," continued the attorney, "what made you think there was some one outside of the house on the ground below the porch who called Mr. Collander to the door?"

The prosecuting attorney was on his feet before the sentence was ended.

"Your Honor," he said, "this thing is ridiculous. Colonel Armant has started in at the end of this case to set up one of the old stock defenses. Your Honor knows 'em; everybody knows 'em; they are the last resort of the guilty; the 'alibi' and the 'mysterious stranger.' He could not use the alibi because everybody saw this woman on the spot. Not even Colonel Armant with all his acuteness could get in an alibi. As it happened, Robert McNagel, the chief of police, was out at the engine house just below Collander's residence. Colonel Armant was there; they were sitting in the engine house when they heard the shots. McNagel ran with the Colonel to Collander's house; they were the first persons on the ground. McNagel was there when the woman ran out of the house and when she shouted, 'Save me, Colonel.' He went after her and brought her back, so the alibi had to be given up. The only thing left is the 'mysterious stranger.'"

The prosecuting attorney laughed.

"Colonel Armant has to get something to make a defense out of. We have shown that this woman had a motive for killing Collander. It is the oldest motive in the world. She lived there as housekeeper. I don't say that other persons did not want to kill him. I have not undertaken to mislead the court about him. Everybody knows our brother Collander was a pretty gay old dog who took a lot of chances on somebody killing him, no doubt. And somebody did kill him, but it was not a 'mysterious stranger.' We have shown who it was. It was the person who had a motive to kill him, the opportunity to kill him, and who not only threatened to do it, but who had prepared a weapon with which to do it. Here are the elements that the law requires; time, place, opportunity, motive and conduct. Why, she as good as said it when McNagel ran after her to bring her back into the house. It was lucky McNagel was on the ground."

The big attorney made an explosive assent.

"It is lucky," he said, "that McNagel was on the ground. It's the very luckiest thing that ever happened."

He turned about toward the prosecuting attorney, now returning to his chair.

"It is true," he said, "I was sitting in the engine house with McNagel when we heard the shots. He ran with me and we were the first persons on the ground. And that reminds me, I want to ask McNagel a question or two just here."

He looked around. The chief of police was sitting in a chair inside the rail, just behind the prosecuting attorney.

He made a motion as though about to rise.

"Don't get up," said the lawyer. "You can answer where you are. Now, Bobby," he said, "we heard two shots close together. They were very close together, were they not?"

"Yes, Colonel," replied the chief of police, "the two shots were fired in rapid succession."

"But there was interval enough," said the lawyer, "for us to be certain that there were two shots."

"That's right, Colonel," replied the chief, "they were close together, but there were two shots; and that was confirmed by the fact that the pistol on the floor had been twice discharged; there were two empty cartridges in it when we picked it up. It had been fired twice."

"Just a moment, Bobby," the lawyer interrupted. "I want to be absolutely certain about this; there could be no mistake about the fact that you heard two shots; isn't that true?"

"Yes, it's true," said the chief, "we heard two shots, there couldn't be any mistake about it."

"Sometimes," said the colonel, "it happens that shots are fired so close together that they make one report. I mean several shots may be fired so rapidly that at a little distance one hears but one report, or so confuses all of the reports that they appear to make but one; isn't that true?"

"Yes, it's true," replied the chief of police. "It happened when Jones was killed over at the power plant, and it happened in our fight with the Lett burglars; I could not say how many times the man had shot at me. I thought he shot at me three times, but he must have shot at me five or six times, for every chamber in his pistol was empty."

"Ah!" said the colonel. "Now, Bobby, that's just exactly what I wanted to find out. Sometimes shots are fired so close together that the most experienced person—a competent person like yourself—could not say whether there was one report or several reports."

The chief of police took hold of the lapels of his coat in either hand and looked at the attorney.

"You have got it right, Colonel. But you are not trying to make out that only one shot was fired on the night Collander was killed, are you?"

The lawyer's face took on an expression of immense surprise.

"Oh, Bobby," he said, "of course not. What I particularly wish to establish, make certain, is that there were two shots close together; but certainly two shots. Now, isn't that absolutely the fact, Bobby? There may have been more shots fired, simultaneously with these—there may have been three shots or four shots—but beyond question, beyond doubt, there were at least two. We heard them; you heard two shots; isn't that right, Bobby?"

"That's right," replied the chief of police, "there were two, sure."

"Bobby," continued the lawyer, "you are chief of police; you and I were the first persons on the ground. You know more about this than anybody else, and your statement about it is worth more than the statements of all other persons put together; now, listen to me carefully and correct me if I make any mistake. Isn't this what happened? You and I, and some of the boys, were sitting in the engine house; we were talking; I was telling you about the Baker case—strangest case in the world—when we heard these shots; one right after the other. I do not know how many, but two certainly. You and I ran up to the Collander residence which stands just across the street from the engine house. As we went in, the prisoner here, Ellen, ran out, and as she ran out she shouted 'Save me, Colonel.' You ran after her to catch her and I went on into the house. By that time Scalley, on the route out here, had come up; you turned the woman over to him and came back. I was standing in the door that led into Collander's study."

The Colonel stopped. He looked intently at the chief of police.

"Now, Bobby," he said, "you won't mind if I say that I have always taken a great deal of interest in you. When you were first appointed I tried to give you the benefit of my experience. I pointed out what ought to be done when a crime was discovered. You are a capable man, Bobby; you saw what I meant and you have profited by it. You know what to do when you get on the scene of a crime. You know how important it is that every precaution shall be taken to preserve the scene of a criminal act, in every detail, precisely as it happened when the crime was discovered; isn't that so, Bobby?"

"Yes, it's so. I don't deny that you put me on to a lot of things and, also, I have learned some for myself. Anyhow, that's right. The first thing to do is to see that everything stays just the way it is."

"Precisely!" replied the attorney. "Now, Bobby, isn't it true that Collander was lying on the floor dead, that his pistol was lying on the floor beside him—two chambers in it empty—and all doors and windows were closed? There were bookcases around the room with glass doors; these were all closed. Now, the first thing you did, Bobby, was to take every precaution to see that all articles in the room should remain precisely as they were found; you put seals on all doors and windows, on all drawers of the tables, and on the doors of the bookcases, so that they would remain closed precisely as they were found. You also carefully chalked on the floor the position of the articles that had to be removed—such, for example, as the weapon and the decedent's body; isn't that precisely true?"

"Yes, it's true, Colonel, that's what I did."

"Now," said the lawyer, "from the appearance of the table in that room was it not evident that Collander was at work on a brief—there was a pad on the table before him, and the papers in the case of the Bridge Company against the Western Railroad? We know that he was at work on this brief because the case was coming on for a hearing, and because his notes on the pad were in ink and the ink was not dry; isn't that true?"

"Yes," replied the chief of police, "that's true."

"Every paragraph written on the pad," the attorney continued, "was part of an opinion from a U. S. Report. It was half of a long syllabus of the opinion; he had it about half written out. As I say, the ink was not yet dry on it; it still blurred a little when one rubbed one's finger on it. Now, we see what the man was doing. He was sitting at the table copying this syllabus when he was interrupted; isn't that true, Bobby?"

"It must have been that way," said the chief of police. "Collander must have been sitting there when the thing began."

The Colonel continued.

"Collander was killed by a bullet that entered the chest and ranged upward. It was found against the shoulder blade, so flattened that no one could say precisely the caliber of the bullet; isn't that true?"

The prosecuting attorney interrupted.

"There's nothing in that, Colonel," he said. "The surgeons say that the bulk of the bullet was about the size of a thirty-two caliber; there was the pistol on the floor from which it had been fired."

The big attorney made a gesture with his hand. "Let us adhere precisely to the truth," he said, "and the truth is that the bullet was so battered that no one can say accurately what caliber it was. Doctor Hull says that he thinks it was a thirty-two, but he also says that he does not know."

The prosecuting attorney persisted.

"But there on the floor was the pistol from which two bullets had been fired."

"Ah!" said the attorney. "Now, we have got to the very point by which the innocence of this prisoner is established. If two bullets were fired in that room, with the doors and windows closed, and one of them killed Collander, where did the other one go that did not kill him?"

He turned to the chief of police. He advanced toward him. His voice became low—became confidential—as of one who discusses a secret, covert, hidden matter with another.

"Now, Bobby," he said, "I directed you to go over that room from top to bottom carefully, every inch of it, precisely as it stood after you had sealed the doors and windows. For what purpose? To determine, Bobby, what became of that other bullet. A bullet cannot vanish. It cannot disappear. It has to hit something. Did you find what it hit?"

The chief of police moved in his chair. His figure lost some aspect of its assurance. He became perplexed. His voice took on a sort of apology. He looked at the judge, at the prosecuting attorney, at the jury.

"I have to tell the truth about it," he said finally. "I couldn't find where that other bullet hit. I never could find it."

"You went over everything in the room, didn't you?" continued the Colonel. "You went over it with Doctor Hull and with Scalley. You went over every inch of it."

"Yes," replied the chief of police, "we went over every inch of it."

"And you didn't find the mark of the bullet?"

The chief of police addressed the judge.

"No, your Honor, we couldn't find it. It's a mystery what became of that other bullet. The person who shot at Collander must have missed him the first time because only one bullet hit him and there were two shots fired. I heard 'em, and there were two empty cartridges in the pistol. Whoever killed him must have shot at him and missed him. But if they did, that bullet had to hit something in the room; and it never hit anything in the room!"

"Ah!" The attorney's voice returned to its normal volume. "You couldn't be mistaken about that, Bobby?"

"No," the chief of police answered, "there can't be any mistake about it. I went over it too carefully, too many times; there's no bullet mark in that room."

He said it with an energy of final decision that dismissed the question conclusively.

The court room was now awake. The packed audience leaned forward. It had now a deep, new interest; the interest of a doubt; the interest of a mystery.

Colonel Armant closed his case at this point.

He had, now, the two elements for which every attorney labors in a desperate criminal defense; a doubt and an involving mystery. The doubt he would build up in his argument, and for the mystery he had the solution ready.

But he was too wise, too greatly a master of effect, to disclose that solution before the proper dramatic moment. He had no intention to permit the attorney for the State to discount his explanation in the opening speech to the jury.

It was after that, when in his argument he had prepared the way, when his defense had been carefully built up, and the state of feeling in the court room—tense and expectant as before a closed door, that he uncovered the solution, like one who, with a magnificent gesture, flings that closed door open.

McNagel could find no bullet mark in the room, because there had been no shot in the room.

The assassin, on that night, had called Collander to the door; he had gone with his own pistol in his hand. And there with the door open, looking out on to the porch, the shooting had occurred.

It had been an instantaneous duel.

Collander had fired twice and the assassin simultaneously with the last report of the pistol. It was this third shot that the prisoner had distinguished.

How clear it was!

Collander was fearful of this thing. He was looking for it to happen; and so he went to the door with the weapon in his hand, and he fired on the instant the menace appeared.

The lawyer reënacted the dramatic scene; the man feeling the impact of the bullet, sprang back, closing the door, then he staggered, the pistol fell out of his hand, he tried to reach his chair, but the wound was mortal, and he lurched, falling behind it, as they had found him.

The confirmatory facts were now conspicuous; no mark of a bullet in the room, and the range of the bullet upward from the assassin standing on the ground below the decedent!

It was an impressive piece of tragic acting. And under its vivid dominance the jury believed themselves to look on at the very act of murder. They saw the thing as it had happened, and the stamp of the attorney's vigor impressed it as with a die.

No array of subsequent argument could dislodge it.

Not guilty, was the verdict within an hour.

* * * *

Colonel Armant and the now vindicated prisoner went out of the court room, down the steps and into his office in the basement of the court house.

The woman sank relaxed into a chair.

"Colonel," she said, "you saved me to-day!"

The lawyer looked at her in surprise.

"Why no," he replied, "I didn't save you to-day!"

His voice descended into its long dwindling whine.

"I saved you, Ellen, when you asked me to save you. While McNagel ran to fetch you I put back into the bookcase the law book from which Collander was copying out the citation for his brief—the law book that he held up before him to ward off your first shot—the bullet-hole is in the cover of it.

"Ellen," he said, "if you had fired down over that book the second time instead of up under it, as you did, I don't know how in hell I could have managed to clear you!"

CHAPTER X

THE INSPIRATION

"Will there be a bobby to hear her scream, north of the Zambezi?"

There were two persons in the room.

It was a small room, looking out over St. James's Park, and attached to the library of the great London house. It was meant for the comfort of one who wished to withdraw from the library in order to examine some book at his leisure, or to make some annotation. There were a table, two comfortable chairs, and a painting, rather large for the room, representing an affair of honor on a snow-covered highway in the rear of a French column, presumably Napoleon's army in Russia.

The conversation between the two persons in the room, Lord Donald Muir and Walker, of the American Secret Service, had passed its preliminary stage.

The youth seated in one of the great chairs was a typical product of the aristocracy of England. He was little more than a boy, but he had already something of the reserve, the almost pretentious restraint, of his race. But he was not entirely within this discipline; an intensity of feeling broke out. It appeared now and then in a word, in an inflection of his voice, in a gesture.

He sat very straight in the chair, in his well-cut evening clothes—his gloves crushed together and gripped in a firm hand that could not remain idle under his intensity of feeling. He was a very good-looking boy, with a single startling feature, his eyebrows were straight and dark, while his hair, weathered by the outdoors, was straw-colored. It gave his blue eyes at all times a somewhat tense expression.

Walker had come to London for a conference with the American Ambassador on the passport forgeries, and he had remained a guest at the Embassy ball. And when the Ambassador had asked him to hear the boy and help him if he could, he had gone with Lord Donald Muir into the little room beyond the great library.

The Ambassador had explained the matter. He had given him each detail; the girl's mother was American; she had married the Earl of Rexford; she was dead; Rexford was dead, and here was this dilemma. Walker knew each of the persons in this drama, especially Sir Henry Dercum, who had been in the English foreign service, and at one time attached to the Embassy in Washington.

Walker was standing, now, before a window, looking out into the night that enveloped London. The boy continued to speak.

"Will he not have the right to take her anywhere he likes?"

The Secret Service agent made a slight gesture, as of one rejecting a suggestion. The gesture was unconscious. The man was thinking of what Lord Donald Muir was saying to him.

"I suppose he has the right to take her anywhere he likes, provided he remains within the jurisdiction of the English law."

"Surely," replied the boy. "Dercum is a clever beast; he will keep within the jurisdiction of the English law."

Walker turned slightly, his face was outlined against the black square of the night framed in the window.

"Then why do you have this fear about it?" he said.

There came a sudden energy into Lord Muir's voice.

"That is all very well as a theory," he said, "but it is quite different in fact.... The English law runs in South Africa; that is the theory. It is a very fine theory, as it used to be lectured into us at the Hill—a great empire providing precisely the same measure of protection for its subject at the most distant point of its dominion that it provided for him in the very capital itself. That is as nearly as I can remember it. It is a fine theory."

"It is a magnificent theory," replied the Secret Service agent, "and England has always endeavored to maintain it."

Lord Muir twisted his gloves; his brown hands gripped them.

"But England can't maintain it; that is the very thing I mean. What protection can the law of England give her in northwestern Rhodesia? The law of England will run there in theory, but it's Dercum's damned will that will run there in fact."

He gripped the gloves suddenly with both hands, as though he were about to destroy them.

"Will there be a bobby to hear her scream?"

He leaned forward in his intensity.

"And what will she be when she comes out? And she won't come out until Dercum's ready. I will tell you what she will be, she will be what Dercum intends her to be."

He looked at the Secret Service agent, his face covered with sweat. Then he continued:

"Do you think this fine English law will do her any good then?"

Walker came a step or two away from the window. He looked down at the boy. His face was composed, with that vague expression it always took on when his interest was very much awakened.

"Sir Henry Dercum," he said, "will have some instincts of a gentleman."

"If he has any instincts of a gentleman," replied the boy, with a sudden energy, "he has kept them so far concealed. London does not know about this man. I have had him looked up. He was unspeakable in Hongkong. No members of the English colony came down to the boat to see him off, although he did represent the empire. But he is a clever beast; one can't get at him.

"I wanted my solicitor to resist his confirmation as guardian, but he said I was not a party in interest."

The boy's voice was charged with an intense vigor.

"I wonder why the law is always so helpless about anything that is important. I had rather see her go to the devil than to Dercum. The devil has a reputation for what he is, and Dercum has a carefully built up reputation in London for what he is not—an explorer, with that sporting instinct that is dear to the English, and a gentleman, when the fact is, he is a crook, a thief when it comes to the accumulation of scientific data, and a bounder! But he is not a fool, and that's what makes him so damnably dangerous; he is infinitely clever."

Walker remained where he had been standing, looking down at the man in the chair, his face in its vague repose. The dilemma of Lord Donald Muir profoundly impressed him.

"I am very much puzzled about this matter," he said. "I cannot say that I trust Dercum, but I can say that I have no reason not to trust him. In fact, he has acted, the American Ambassador tells me, with extreme delicacy. The property which the girl takes from her mother lies in America. He has made no effort to exercise any control over it; he has, in fact, advised the Ambassador that he would be pleased to have the trustees of her mother's estate continue to administer this property until the girl comes of age to receive it. That did not sound like a man with a design.

"It was quite possible for him to obtain the sale of this property in America and the transfer of the funds into his custody under the English law, but he takes the other course. This does not seem precisely consistent with your estimate of the man."

There was a note as of a bitter laugh under Lord Muir's answer.

"It's precisely consistent with my estimate of him. What the brute's after is the girl; when he gets her, he will get everything with her. Why hurry? When Dercum has degraded her enough, he will get all the rest of it; he knows what he is doing."

The boy got up suddenly.

"And I can't stop him," he said, "unless I go and kill him; and the beast is too clever to be killed except in the nastiest way. 'The duel has gone out with the lace coat,' he laughs at me with his little reptilian eyes under the heavy eyelids. 'Have a bit of patience, my boy; I have no objection to you, if you please my ward. But you must wait a little; she is quite young. It is admirable to be youthful and impetuous, but it makes life difficult for a guardian.' That's what he says. And I know what he thinks, and I know what he is going to do."

The Secret Service agent interrupted:

"What, precisely?"

"It will be just what I told you a moment ago," replied Lord Muir. "He is laying plans now; she's quite keen to get into any queer corner of the earth. It is easy enough to get a girl worked up, especially when she has a big legend of her father before her. He will do precisely what I have said, take her into South Africa."

He got up with sudden energy.

"The law can't stop him, but there must be something, and that's why I come to you, sir," he added.

"To me," said Walker, "—because you believe in providence?"

"Yes, sir," the boy continued, "that is precisely the reason I came to you. It is true that the American Ambassador has a point of attack with Dercum because of these American properties, but that is not the thing I depended upon. My uncle, when he was chief of the criminal investigation department of Scotland Yard, used to say when we had a perplexed thing to take up with America: 'We can unravel it, if Captain Walker comes up with one of his inspirations from heaven.' Well, sir, I have come to you for one of these inspirations."

Walker laughed softly. The reputation was perhaps his greatest asset—a sort of intuition arising at certain complicated stages of an affair, the sudden swift realization of some essential hitherto unobserved.

Walker continued to smile.

The young man was looking at him with a tense, serious expression.

"You will have one of these inspirations, Captain Walker?"

The Secret Service agent began to walk about the room.

He was disturbed that Lord Donald Muir should come to him with this affair. It was not a thing in which he ought to take any part. Outside of some courteous discussion at the request of the American Ambassador, he did not see how it was possible for him to have anything to do with the matter. And further, it disturbed him that this youth should come depending upon what was to him the absurd phase of a detective reputation.

Scotland Yard called his sudden swift insight into some complicated matter, "the inspirations from heaven of the Chief of the American Secret Service," and not precisely with a complimentary accent. The thing annoyed him. But he smiled at the youth in the chair—that vague, placid smile for which the man was famous.

"I do not see what I can do, my dear Lord Muir," he said; "but I shall be receptive to any inspiration that may arrive. Let us go down."

They went out of the little room into the great library.

It was a long, immense room, and the doors were closed. As they passed through, the music from below ascended, and the vast confusion of human voices, like the hum of some distant insect hive. Walker opened the door, and they were at once above an immense sea of human figures, gay, brilliant.

The crowded Embassy ball moved below them. The jewels, the gowns of women, the color of uniforms gave the thing the aspect of an almost barbaric saturnalia. The dense crowd overflowed onto the bronze stairway.

Lord Muir entered and was lost in the immense throng, seeking the one about whom he was so greatly concerned. The Chief of the American Secret Service went slowly down the stairway, moving his hand along the mahogany rail under which, in a magnificent frieze, a wood-nymph entangled in a flowering vine fled from the pursuit of satyrs. He was more disturbed than he had been willing to admit.

This girl was the daughter of that charming American woman who had married the Earl of Rexford.

Captain Walker had not cared greatly for the Earl of Rexford; he was too typically an Englishman, following conventions that seemed a trifle out of modern times; but he was compelled, in a measure, to admire him. While other men wasted their fortunes in the frivolities of London, this man had spent what he could get in exploration, in fitting out expeditions to discover unknown places of the earth. And he went with them, enduring the hardship and peril.

He had died in his greatest venture. The whole expedition had perished on one of the wind-swept plateaus of the Antarctic. It was Dercum who had gone in to find him, and he had found him frozen to death—the very dogs frozen, in one of those fearful depressions of temperature that sometimes descend in an immense blizzard on this wind-swept plateau.

From Dercum's report he had very nearly reached Rexford alive. The expedition had evidently held out for days against the blizzard. The Earl of Rexford had been the last man to go. In the snow hut, on the canvas table, was his diary, written up. Beside it, on the blank sheet, were a dozen paragraphs in which he had directed the appointment of Dercum as guardian for his minor daughter, with all custody and direction of his estate.

The Secret Service agent passed these things through his mind as he descended—the brilliant laughter, the murmur of voices below, making a swirl of noises. He remembered some of the details arising in the formal matter of Dercum's appointment after his return. A solicitor or some official authority had ventured a doubt about the handwriting on the page beside the last entry in the diary. But it was shown to him that the writing of innumerable pages of the diary varied, due to the cold or to the physical condition of the writer at the time.

The persons in Dercum's expedition, persons whose integrity could not be doubted, had been but a few minutes behind him in entering this snow hut in which the Earl of Rexford had been found, and they had at once, at Dercum's direction, written their signatures at the bottom of the page.

The diary had been immediately authenticated. It could not have been afterward changed. And it was shown that these signatures, written in that immense cold by benumbed fingers, varied from the normal signatures of the individuals returning to their common environment of life. In fact, no one could have said who had written these signatures if the men who had written them that day, at Dercum's direction, in the snow hut on the canvas table, had not been present in England to establish the fact. The diary, the ink, the pen were there on the canvas table, and these men had established by their signatures the authenticity of this writing beyond question.

At this moment a tall man wearing a distinguished order passed the Chief of the American Secret Service.

"Sir," he said, "are you perhaps receiving an inspiration from heaven on our Hyde Park murders?"

Walker smiled.

"It would be my only hope," he said, "against the superior intelligence of Scotland Yard."

And he went on. He was annoyed by the incident. Would he never escape from this ridiculous pretension!

As he entered the crowd overflowing on the bottom of the stairway, he caught a glimpse of Sir Henry Dercum and the girl in an eddy beyond where the great newel post turned. Dercum's big shoulders would be anywhere conspicuous. He was a massive Englishman, with a wide, Oriental face, purpled by good feeding, and little reptilian eyes under heavy lids that very nearly obscured them. The man had a habit of lifting his head when he was very much concerned, as though to get a better view of his subject without the effort or the danger of raising his eyelids.

The girl before him was in the splendid lure of youth; her dark hair was lifted, by some subtlety of the coiffeur's art, into a beautiful, soft background for her face; her dark eyes and her delicate skin were exquisitely brought out by it. She was in the first bud of life, and she was very lovely.

But there was more than mere physical beauty; there was the charm of inexperience, the charm of adventurous youth that does not question, and, like charity, believeth all things—that inexperience which is gayly ready for any adventure into what it beautifully imagines to be a fairy world.

The Secret Service agent saw the expression bedded into Dercum's heavy face, and he knew what it meant. He heard also the sentence he was speaking.

"You will need a bit of change from all this artificiality."

"Do I look stale so soon, Sir Henry?"

The girl laughed.

His eyes traveled over her, his head thrown back in a slow, heavy-lidded expression as though it were a physical caress.

"Ah, no," he said; "but you will have inherited some of your father's interest in the waste places of the earth. How would you like to go with me and find a lost river?"

"I should love it," she said. "Where is your lost river, Sir Henry?"

He looked about him.

"Let us find a seat somewhere," he said, "and I will show you a map."

They got out of the crowd, traversed the long hall that runs parallel to St. James's Park, and entered the conservatory.

Walker followed. Dercum's words had almost the sting of a blow. It was the verification of Lord Donald Muir's anxiety. If love were blind, Walker reflected, it had surely the intuition of the saints. Dercum's plan, the plan which Walker had considered academic and unlikely, was practical and on the way.

The Chief of the American Secret Service went on into the conservatory, through fringes of the gay crowd floating everywhere like gorgeous butterflies disentangled from the mass. He stopped beside an immense vase filled with Japanese chrysanthemums of a peculiar color, huge like a shock of hair on an immense stem. They entirely obscured him, and he did not move.

It was not in any definite plan that he had entered the conservatory and stopped behind this mass of flowers. He had been surprised, shocked by the swift verification of this boy's fear, and he wished to reflect on it. It was not that he had followed to hear what Dercum said; the details of what he said would be now unimportant. It was the man's intention alone that mattered, and this intention required no further explanatory word.

He felt a sudden and desperate anxiety. This girl, lovely and inexperienced, was entirely at Dercum's will; as her guardian he would have exclusive control of her, and, with the man's cleverness, what he wished he would accomplish. The English law, having put the girl into his charge, would not concern itself about intentions that could not be established. It would concern itself only with the overt act, and when Dercum resorted to that he would be beyond a running of the King's writ.

Walker felt himself pressed for reflection, and he stopped here unmoving, without a plan. But as chance would have it, he stopped precisely at the place he would have selected if he had followed in determination to hear every word that Dercum was about to say. Sir Henry and the girl were just beyond him—beyond the screen of flowers, on a bench by the window. Their words, although under-uttered, came clearly to him; and in his vague reflection, the skill with which Dercum moved in his plan was conspicuously evident.

The man was getting the lure of a land of mystery into his story; he was deftly stimulating the girl's fancy; he was calling her interest in her father's adventures to his aid; he was making a wonder expedition out of this thing he had in mind. No element of thrill, or color, in this adventure was lacking.

Walker could almost see Dercum's finger on the map. But the map would be only a property of the thing he was staging. He did not explain precisely where this river lay, or the route to it. But on some golden afternoon they would unship at a seaport, assemble a fantastic company and go into some lost country that would be like the Wood beyond the World, or the waste regions of some fairy kingdom. And they would go now, this very summer, when the London season had slacked a little.

Dercum was beginning to specify dates. Walker could not see him, but he knew that the bit of pencil moved on the map; he would arrange everything. From the few words of the girl, reaching him across the Japanese chrysanthemums, she was entranced. A butterfly entangled in illusions— she was ready to go, and she would go.

And with his clear vision, the vision not accustomed to be obscured by detail, the Chief of the American Secret Service saw that the thing could not be prevented. One could interfere with the custody of a guardian only with an established intent in an English court. This intent must be based on evidence, and there would be no evidence; there would not be even the knowledge that the thing was contemplated. With infinite cleverness Dercum had drawn the girl into a conspiracy of silence. They would arrange it; they would keep their own counsels, and they would go. It would have all the secret, alluring charm of a fairy adventure.

Walker heard the pledge of silence, and knew that they were coming out. He saw, also, looking down the long hall toward the drawing-room, Lord Donald Muir advancing in his search. He would be here in a moment; the three of them would meet, in a moment, just beyond where he stood behind the chrysanthemums. Already Dercum and the girl were very nearly up to him.

What would he do?

There was something surely to be done. The world behind its harsh, indifferent machinery must be controlled by some immense considerate impulse. All the operations of life could not be abandoned to a mere physical fatalism, to laws that were unthinking, or to a tendency that could not change. There must be something in the universe to interfere against the iniquity of human intentions and this indifference of nature! And suddenly, with a flash of vision, Walker saw what had happened in Rexford's snow hut, on the plateau of the Antarctic, during the twenty minutes that Dercum had been there before his expedition had come up—he saw it as clearly as though he had been looking on.

He called to Lord Donald Muir, and he advanced to meet Dercum and the girl.

"Sir Henry," he said, "will you release these young people to the dance and walk a moment with me?"

Dercum lifted his big Oriental face, looking out under his heavy eyelids. He moved the tips of the girl's fingers to his lips, and he nodded to Muir.

"You will be a very brilliant couple," he said. "I shall be charmed to observe you."

And then he turned to the Chief of the American Secret Service.

"Ah, Walker," he said, "I have not seen you since the old days in Washington."

The Chief of the American Secret Service put his hand through Dercum's arm and drew him along beside him, down the hall, with an ease of manner as though he were the warm companion of a lifetime.

"My friend," he said, "I am going to ask you to release this guardianship and go on your expedition alone."

Dercum stopped suddenly, his body rigid.

"You have overheard," he said.

Walker smiled. He made a slight gesture.

"It is one of the perquisites of the Secret Service," he said. "You will grant my request, Sir Henry."

"Your request?" Dercum's voice was almost a stutter. "I grant it?"

The Chief of the American Secret Service took a firmer hold of his arm.

"Walk with me," he said; "we may be noticed.... Ah, yes, my friend, you will grant it."

"Why should I grant it, pray?" said the amazed Dercum.

"You will grant it," replied Walker, "because you will not wish to answer in the English courts—in the English criminal courts—a question that has just occurred to me."

The Chief of the American Secret Service laughed; two persons connected with a Continental Embassy were regarding him. Then he went on:

"How did it happen, Sir Henry, that when you came on Lord Rexford's expedition on the Antarctic plateau, that morning, when you entered his snow hut some twenty minutes ahead of the other members of your expedition, and in that low temperature, in that deadly Antarctic temperature, you found everything frozen, the food, the very mercury in the thermometer, the bodies of the dead—how did it happen, Sir Henry"—and his hand moved on Dercum's arm like a caress—"how did it happen that the ink on the canvas table was not also frozen?"

CHAPTER XI

THE GIRL IN THE PICTURE

I advanced to meet the man with a sense of victory. The United States Secret Service had searched the world for him. He had been long concealed. But my sense of victory vanished when I saw him.

He sat in a great chair on the long terrace that overlooked the sweep of lawn and the dark, rapid river. He had been, all the time, under our very noses. We had thought of every other place except an English country house within a jump of London. And he had been sitting here in every comfort that money could assemble.

He did not rise when I was brought out to him.

He leaned back in the chair, lifted his heavy face, and laughed!

"And so," he said, "you finally wormed it out of her."

I could not keep my voice level—so effectively was the man escaping us after all this search.

And I did not know what the huge creature meant. On the night before, some one had called up Scotland Yard and said our man was here; the English Secret Service was giving us all the aid it could. The call from some shop in Regent Street could not be traced—so it had been a woman! I replied as though I were in his secret.

"She knew you were safe."

He laughed again. "Sure, she knew it!"

He pointed to a chair a few feet beyond him across a table.

"Sit down," he said. "I want to talk about her—that's the reason I wanted you to come." He laughed again. "You thought you'd sleuthed it out, eh? Not by a jugful. I sent her word to put you wise. I wanted to clear some things up before I cashed in. But it was a clean lie. What I wanted was somebody to listen while I talked about her. Sit down."

It was a strange introductory. But it was a mystery that had puzzled everybody, and I was willing to hear all that he had to say about it. I took the chair beyond him.

He shot his head forward suddenly, in a tense gesture.

"She's a heavenly angel!" he said. "I don't know what God Almighty meant by setting her in the game with the bunch of crooks that He's got running the world—unless He counted on me." The laugh became a sort of chuckle in his big throat—"Ain't she a heavenly angel?"

He whipped a worn photograph out of his pocket and reached it across the table to me.

It was the photograph of a girl with a narrow slit cut out across the face. It had been taken from a painting; one could tell from the flat surface. A strange background of beauty and an indescribable charm in the pose of the girl remained even in the mutilated picture.

"I cut the face," he added, "so she wouldn't come into the case if you caught me; your little Westridge must have been slaughtered at the loss of her."

Again he touched me at an unexpected point.

Shortly after the thing had happened, Lord Westridge returned to England. He had come to visit some rich Americans, and there was a rumor that some adventure had befallen him. Nothing definite ever came to me, and I liked the man too little to inquire; all the blood from the original Glasgow solicitor would "bite a shilling." But again I replied as though I were in his secret.

"What happened to Westridge?" I said.

The man twisted around in his chair.

"Friend," he said, "you've got a head full of brains or you wouldn't be Chief of the United States Secret Service; now answer me a question—What's the biggest notion in the Christian Church?"

"I don't know," I answered him truthfully.

"Well, I know," he went on. "It's the notion that you'll get what's a-comin' to you!"

He looked at me with a big, cynical leer.

"That's what happened to your little Westridge—and the next time you see him he's a-goin' to get another jolt. He will be damned sorry that you found me. He couldn't squeal, any place along the line, but I'll bet a finger he didn't let Scotland Yard forget about me."

And again I saw an incident of this long search, for the man before me, from another angle. The Blackacre Bank had kept the search hot for him, pretending the public welfare. I saw it now, that was Westridge's money box—that would be little Westridge in the background.

He eyed me curiously in a moment's pause.

"He kept slippin' you the word, eh? Well, she blocked him at that, even if she didn't know it."

There came a sudden energy into his voice.

"An' if the plague hadn't got me I'd 'a' saved her that trouble; I'd 'a' played ring-a-round-a-rosy with you."

He lifted himself in the chair with the strength of his hands on the broad arm-rests. And I realized more fully what a physical wreck he was—the lower part of his body was motionless.

"I want to tell you about this thing," he said. "And then you can go ahead with your warrant."

"I fear," I replied, "that a somewhat higher authority has got in before the King's writ."

He chuckled as though the deadly fact were a sort of pleasantry.

"Sure," he said, "the big Judge has beat you to it."

He looked out, a moment, at the woolly Highland cattle in the distant meadow, at the age-old beech-trees and the dark, swift, silent water, and then the upper part of his big body settled in the chair.

"I thought it was a slick trick, but maybe it was God Almighty. Anyway when the thing was pulled off I slid up to Bar Harbor and set down in a hotel. I figured it out like this—you look for a crook in the places that crooks go, and you look for a gentleman in the places where gentlemen go. I'll switch it.

"I got me some quiet clothes. I limped a little to show that I wasn't golf-fit and I didn't talk. I just set about with the New York *Times* and the *Financial Register* and let the days pass. When there was doings in the hotel I was there in my all-right evening clothes, in a chair against the wall, and I limped along the sea path in the afternoon for a little exercise.

"I looked some bored to keep the proper form. But I wasn't bored. I was seeing something new and I was getting more light on it all the time.

"I was seeing that this bunch was living up to a standard that nearly all the people I'd ever seen were only pretending. That was the difference, I soon figured it out."

He flung up his hand in a curious, expressive gesture.

"I'm a crook, keep that in your head, and the thing was like a theater to me. I began to watch the actors; then I saw *her* and Westridge."

He moved in his chair.

"She was there with an old faded grandmother that read novels and smoked cigarettes—and was a lady. And right there is where this real bunch has got the goods! They don't let down because they do some things that would make you cross your fingers on the other set."

He leaned back in the chair.

"Well! I got to watching her and your Englishman. I watched them dancing in the hotel, and riding, and playing tennis at the Casino—I'd never seen any people like them.

"And pretty soon I got on to something; this Westridge gentleman was trying to buy the girl, but he didn't want to pay for her. He was putting out the bait, but he had a string to it.

"I got on to his dope.

"If he could dazzle her into marrying him she'd get her board and clothes. The real thing that was next to his hide was his money. 'All for *me*,' that was the notion."

He went on with no break in his words.

"I got to thinking about it. This little Westridge was forty; he'd never change; and the girl was at the age when the things he was dangling were all mixed up with moonshine. He might win, and if he did she was headed for hell.

"I saw it all clean out to the end."

He moved in the chair.

"I used to set about, and look at her, and it made me cold all over. The devil was on the job right here just as he was in the Tenderloin. He was working on a higher-class line, but it was only a different sort of road to his same old hell.

"It would be a heavenly angel flung to a wolf no matter how you dressed the situation up; an' I said to myself, 'You can't beat him. The devil's got a set of traps for any kind of a layout!'"

He lifted himself on his great hands and turned the whole of his body toward me.

"Now," he said, "what's the difference how you ruin a woman? When you got the job finished, ain't it finished? If you string it out over a dozen years and kill everything nice and generous and lovely in her with your little, contemptible 'all for *me*' meanness, inside of a preacher's permit, ain't you ruined her, just the same as if you'd white-slaved her? And ain't it the same motive, 'all for *me*,' darn the difference?

"I tell you," he shook the arms of the chair in his great hands, "the thing begun to get my goat. Her father, a lawyer in the South, was dead. She had only the old Boston grandmother (I heard the talk among the women) and the coin was getting scarce. Your little Englishman played in form, every point correct, and he was goin' to get her.

"I seen it!

"She was standing before the hotel desk with the bill that the clerk puts in your box at the end of the week, when his big motor snorted in against the wooden steps. Your little Westridge understood it for the grin started. It was the same old grin that goes with the job—I've seen it on all of 'em.

"An' that settled it!"

His voice became cold, level, even like a metallic click.

"'Now, my little gentleman,' I said to myself, 'we'll just see if you do! Right here is where "Alibi Al" sets in with a stack of blues.'

"I got up, folded my newspaper, and took a turn up and down the veranda, as though I was trying out my game leg, an' then I limped down to the fashionable church just across from the library.

"I stepped up inside the door."

He paused, and his voice changed to its former note.

"You see I had to have a little help on this job. It had a big loose end.

"I went in and sat down in a pew. It was dim and quiet and I got right down to business. I didn't run in any of the prayer-book curtain-raisers. I put the thing right up to the boss.

"'Now, look here, Governor,' I said, 'has a helpless little girl got a pull with you, or is it bunk? Because I'm a-goin' to call you, and if the line your barkers are putting out is on the level, you've got to come across with the goods. If there's nothing to it, the Government ought to shut 'em up on a fraud order—I'm a-goin' to carry one end of this thing; get busy at the other end!'

"Then I went out.

"That night I went over to see little Westridge.

"They'd been to dinner at Jordan's Pond and had come in early. Westridge wasn't in the hotel; he was stopping with the Lesterfields; a big, gray stone house facing the sea. The butler showed me in. There wasn't anybody about but Westridge. The Lesterfields were down at Newport.

"He was surprised to see me—didn't understand it; he'd never met me in the social line. But it was America where anything might happen, even a man come to see you that you hadn't been introduced to."

The speaker paused to move one of his knees; he lifted it with his hands.

"I didn't waste any time cutting brush before Mr. Westridge. I went right in to what I had to say. My line was: friend of the girl's father, blunt old Western business man, no manners, and don't give a cuss for you. Easy stuff, you see, and the kind of thing your Englishman expects in the 'States.'

"He was mighty formal, as you'd say, but he didn't throw any stuttering into Alibi Al. I set down, just as if the place belonged to me, and I waved a hand at him. I said to myself, 'You're a little piker; line up and take what's coming to you.'

"But what I said out loud was like this,

"'Carrots has got a little bunch of stuff that's goin' to be wiped out if it ain't covered.'

"That was her nickname among the youngsters, because her blue-black hair in the sun had a heavenly copper glint.

"He looked mixed up.

"'What, precisely, do you mean?' he says.

"I didn't pay any attention to him. I went on just as if he hadn't said a word.

"'Women's got no sense about business—she's agoin' to lose it?'

"'Lose what?' he says.

"'Rotten the way they bring girls up,' I says, the same as if he hadn't spoke. 'Here's this steel bunch beating the stuff down; her broker wires for somethin' to cover it, an' she sticks the telegram up against the lookin'-glass so she'll remember to write to him next week—can you beat it?'

"I saw everything that was goin' through him, same as if you'd rolled it out on the picture reel.

"The 'old friend, no manners, darn the difference' stuff had hooked him. And there were two other hooks: this girl had some property that he didn't know of, and the friends of the family, like me, was a-coming to him about it.

"Because what?

"Because it was settled stuff on our side that she was goin' to take his arm up the church aisle. It was the first straight dope he'd had, an' it bucked him, same as it bucked me to know that she was dangling him with no word passed.

"He set up now pleasant as you please.

"'Ah—er, yes,' he says; he hadn't got the name I was playing under.

"I bellowed at him, an' he mighty near jumped.

"'Johnson!' I said. 'Alonzo Johnson, Kansas City!'

"'Quite so, Mr. Johnson,' he says, quick, same as you'd apologize, 'there's some business affair to discuss, I fauncy?'

"He fell right in with the line of dope mighty easy and comfortable. You see it was something like the way they do things up in his country. The old uncle or the family lawyer calls on you, when ma thinks that things are pretty well understood with the young people, and gits down to figgerin'. It was near enough to my line to go across with him. He knew that the girl hadn't got any men folk, so an old friend of the family would fit the form as a sort of next-of-kin, as the law-books say."

The big man linked his fingers together on the chair arm.

"As I was sayin', he walked right in and made himself at home with the notion. He called her 'Carrots' straight back at me; it was 'Kiss her, pap; she's our'n now,' and he begun to grin.

"On the soul of Satan, man, it was all I could do to keep my foot away from him. I wanted to hoist him out of that chair and skite him around among the furniture—but I had to keep my poker face on.

"He bounced up and got a box of cigars and a little dish full of matches and shoved them across the table. I took one, bit the end off, scratched the match on my foot, lighted it, and went ahead.

"'It's the butt end of what she's got,' I says, 'an' it's in the door.'

"He knew all about business, and he picked the things right out.

"'You mean,' he says, 'that her solicitor has invested her fortune in a stock on margin and the market is declining?'

"'You got it,' I says, 'only she done it herself, on some tip from her swell friends.'

"'How extraordinary!' he piped; his voice got thin when it hit money. 'Is it a legitimate stock?'

"'Sure,' I answered, 'one of the six good ones.' I didn't know how many good ones there was.

"'Why does it decline?' His voice went up like a singing school.

"'The steel bunch are clubbing it,' I says.

"He understood that, and began to finger around his little wax mustache.

"'Quite so,' he cheeped, 'quite so.' Then he squared toward me.

"'Ah—er, Mr. Johnson,' he says, 'I fauncy you came with some plan about it.'

"'Plan nothin',' I says; 'the stuff's got to be covered—they'll git it beat under her figger in another day's poundin'.'

"'Ah—er—quite so,' he was cool as a julep; 'you are intending, I fauncy, to cover the margin?'

"I leaned over the table and blew a mouthful of smoke on him.

"'Sure!' I roared in his face, 'if I can get fifty thousand dollars, quick.'

"He ducked out of the smoke.

"'That's a very large sum of money,' he says.

"I lolled over the table an' smoked on him like a Dutch uncle.

"'Big money!' I gurgled it, like a man choking on a laugh. 'Do you know how much Carrots has got hanging on it?'

"He didn't answer that; I knew he wouldn't.

"'Where, precisely, do you expect to get this money?' he says.

"I set up more calm like at that.

"'Well,' I says, 'I thought maybe we could raise it together.'

"He wanted that fake fortune saved for him, so it would come along with the girl, but he wanted somebody else to carry the chance.

"I knew it, and I smoked on him. I hung over the table and puffed it in his face. He tried to duck out of it, and I followed him around. It done me good. I couldn't spit on the little tightwad.

"'Now, look here, Mr. Westridge,' I says, 'don't you get a wrong notion in your head; I'm not a-goin' to let you take any risk on this. I'm a-goin' to take the risk; there ain't none, in fact; the stuff's got to bounce back. It'll go to the sky when the steel bunch get all they can grab of it. But whatever risk there may be,' I sputtered it out on him, 'is *mine*. I'll put up the backing an' you get me the money by to-morrow at noon.' I was nearly across the table, an' I didn't wait for him to cut in with a question. I took a big envelope out of my pocket and flashed the stuff on him. He came up with a chirp.

"'My word!' he says, 'where did you get this?'

"'Well,' I answered, 'London's a big selling point with us—you can't trade with the English and not take their stuff, can you? The Johnny whose name's on that stuff put it up with me—same as I'm putting it up with you. There's fourteen of them. Ain't they good for fifty thousand?'"

"He spread the certificates out on the table and run his fingers over them. It was old-fashioned love-touchin'.

"'Oh!' his voice flickered up, 'beyond question.'

"'Done!' I says. 'Keep it until I come back with your money—an' get me the cash before noon to-morrow.'

"'Don't you want a memorandum?' he says.

"I waved my hand, careless, like it was nothin'.

"'That's all right,' I says; 'I don't want any promises about that, but there is a thing that I do want a promise about.'

"I threw my cigar in the fireplace and set down.

"'I want you to promise me that you won't ever say anything to Carrots about this, nor to anybody; it's between us—she's a high-strung youngster,' I added; 'this thing's got to be buried with us, no matter what happens. Is it a trade?'

"We shook hands on it and I got out.

"Before twelve the next day he sent me a draft on New York for the money—an' I'd won a lap."

The afternoon sun lay on the terrace of the gray stone house, where the big creature, dead to the middle, talked from his chair, clearing the mystery that had covered his disappearance from the world. It was an extraordinary story, and I wished to get it, in detail, precisely clear.

"It was fiction," I asked, "this explanation to Westridge?"

He looked at me in a sort of wonder.

"Sure," he said. "I made it up."

"There wasn't any of it true?"

"Not a word," he answered. "Don't you understand? This was a little game that me and God Almighty was settin' up on the side."

"You knew nothing of the girl's affairs?" The thing seemed incredible to me.

"That's right," he replied, "not a thing, except that her father, a lawyer in the South, was dead, and the small coin was beginning to mean some-thing—an' of course the little game of this Westridge person—it was a blind pool; nobody in on it but God Almighty."

I could not forbear a comment.

"He seems to have helped you in the opening."

The big creature turned heavily toward me.

"With little Westridge?" There was deep irony in his voice. "I didn't need any help to handle him. That was ABC stuff. The big trouble was ahead."

"With the girl?" the query escaped me.

"No," he replied; "that was my job too. You listen. I'm comin' to it.

"I looked out for a chance to get the girl by herself, an' about four o'clock I got it. There had been a fog in; it cleared a little and she went for a walk. She took the path along the sea toward Cromwell's Harbor and I followed her. She turned back where the path ends at the harbor, and just before a big house, that hadn't been opened that season, I met her.

"I stopped in the path.

"'Missie,' I said, 'could I speak to you a minute?'

"There was no sham business about her. She was clean and straight and afraid of nothin', like an angel of God.

"'Certainly,' she said. 'What is it, sir?'

"'It's about something I owe to your father,' I said.

"She looked me straight in the face.

"'My father's executor, Mr. Lewis, would be the one to see,' she said. 'I know nothing about business.'

"'It ain't business,' I said, 'it's honor. Could I walk along with you a step?'

"'Why, yes,' she answered, 'if you like.'"

The big man moved his loose bulk in the chair.

"I know something about stories," he said. "I've had to make 'em up so a jury would believe 'em, an' I done my best as I limped along by her.

"'I ain't always been rich,' I says. 'I was down an' out in the eighties, an' I was a-goin' to do somethin' that would have ruined me, when by God's luck I met Harry in Louisville.' (I'd heard the old women call her father Harry, so I had that much to go on.)

"'Al,' he says, 'what's the trouble?'

"I suppose it was in my face. I was broke down an' I told him. He got it all in his head, an' then he patted me on the shoulder. 'Old man,' he said, 'a little money ain't goin' to do you any good. I'll get you fifty thousand dollars an' you go out to the race course this afternoon an' pick a winner.'

"I tried to turn it down. I didn't want to lose his money, I didn't know one horse from another. But he just laughed and kept patting me on the back. 'A beginner for luck,' he says. 'Where's your nerve, Al?' Well, I picked that big Dercum colt that nobody had ever heard of, a five-to-one shot, an' he romped in!

"I was a-limpin' along the sea-path, a-proddin' the gravel with my cane an' a-talkin' to my feet, same as if I was afraid the recollection would get away with me if I wasn't careful. The girl didn't say nothin' and I went on.

"'Harry wouldn't touch the winnin's; he picked out his fifty thousand and put me out of the room.'

"I limped on, talking to my feet.

"'And it saved me two ways, for the thing I was agoin' to do would have ruined me.'

"My voice got down pretty near in a whisper.

"'I never saw Harry after that,' I says, 'until last night.'

"She stopped quick, an' I went on a step or two.

"'My father?' she said.

"'Yes,' I says, not looking up, 'Harry, just as he looked that morning in Louisville—only he was troubled.'

"Then I turned on her like I was makin' a clean breast of it. I had the tears startin' and the right choke-up, an' it wasn't all jury dope. I didn't want that heavenly angel fouled over by little Westridge. It balled the heart out of me.

"'Now, Missie,' I said, 'you've got to help me even this thing up. I don't know nothin' about your affairs—I don't want to know. But you've got to take that same bunch of money and chance it on something.'

"She shook her head, and I had a bad hour. All along that sea-path, with the fog dodging in and out, I kept right at her; I never lost a step. I was old and rich; money was nothin' to me. I didn't have a soul in the world. I couldn't take it with me, an' I couldn't face 'Harry' with the debt hanging over—'Have a heart! have a heart!' That was my line of dope. I was pleading for myself—an' it was the only line that ever would have got her.

"'But what should I do with the money?' she said finally, in a sort of queer hesitation.

"'I'll tell you that to-night,' I answered."

The huge creature seemed to relax, as though there had been a vital tension in the mere memory of the thing.

"That cleaned up my end of it," he continued, "and after dinner when it was getting a little dark, I limped over to the church. I had the last copy of the *Financial Register* in my hand. I stopped in the door. The church was closed and it was dark, but I didn't need any light for the business I come on.

"'Governor,' I says, 'the rest of this job's up to you. I'm a-goin' to open this magazine here in the dark and the first thing that's advertised at the top of the page on the right-hand side is the thing I'm a-goin' to tell her to put the coin on—Ready,' I says, 'go to it!' and I folded back the page and went over to the hotel."

Again he paused.

"I got a jolt when I saw the page. It was some sort of Canadian gold mine, so fishy that the letters had scales on 'em. But I says to myself, 'That's the Governor's business,' an' I cut it out, put it into an envelope with the draft, and left it at the desk for her."

He paused.

"The next morning I slid out. Eight months later the plague struck me. I crippled into England, asked her to hide me while I died, and she put me here."

"And the gold stock," I said, "I suppose it turned her out a fortune?"

The energy came back for an instant into his voice.

"It was so rotten," he replied, "that the Governor General of Canada summoned all the victims to meet with him for a conference in Montreal."

At this moment I caught the sound of a motor entering the gates at some distance through the park. The huge paralytic also heard it, and his attention was no longer toward me. It was on the great coach-colored limousine drawing up at the end of the avenue of ancient beech trees.

I looked with him.

A girl helped out by footmen stepped down into the avenue, carpeted now with the yellow autumn leaves. Even at the distance it was impossible to mistake her; her charm, her beauty were the wonder of England. And on the instant, as in a flash of the eye, I recalled the painted picture hanging in the great house in Berkeley Square, the picture from which this creature's mutilated photograph had been taken, the picture of a young girl, in an ancient chair, with no ornament but a bit of jade on a cord about her neck.

"It's the young Duchess of Hurlingham," I said.

The big creature beside me was struggling to rise, his voice in an excited flutter.

"Sure," he said, "God Almighty didn't throw me down. When she went up to that conference in Montreal, He had young Hurlingham on the spot—fine, straight, clean youngster as ever was born. It was love her at sight; an' now"—he made a great gesture as though to include something without a visible limit—"she's got all these places in England, an' all that Standard Oil money that belonged to his mother's people."

The girl, radiant as a vision, was advancing on the carpet of golden beech leaves, and I hastened to put a final query, the thing I had come here to find out. I had given up the idea of an arrest. The man was dying.

"What did you do with the registered bonds that you got when you cracked the vault of the British Embassy in Washington the night before you went to Bar Harbor? They had Lord Dovedale's name on them, and they could not be negotiated."

The whole sagging body of the unsteady creature strained toward the advancing vision as toward an idol. His voice reached me, stuttering as with fatigue.

"That's the stuff I put up with Westridge for the loan—go and take it away from him!"

CHAPTER XII

THE MENACE

We never could persuade Walker to discuss his adventures in enforcing the prohibition Amendment: perhaps because the methods of the service were in use and could not be revealed.

But one night, when we pressed him, he took the proofs of a magazine story out of a locked file and gave them to us.

"Here," he said, "is the great peril to the Amendment. We had to suppress the whole magazine issue to get this story out. Of course the elements in this story are fictitious, but on any day they may become an appalling reality."

We read the story. And here it is:

"Five Millions is a Big Sum of Money."

"Sure, it's a big sum of money. But I'm going to do this thing up right! You heard me wishin' the other day that I could double cross the bunch of cranks that's a-runnin' this country. Well, I've done stopped wishin'. I'm goin' to do something to double-cross 'em. You hear what I say, Stetman! I'm a-goin' to offer five millions of dollars to any chemist who can find the active principle in alcohol!"

The attorney, tall, angular, incisive, did not move.

Arnbush pounded on the table with his fat clenched hand.

"The rest of the bunch can keep on wishin' and startin' little lawsuits. I'm goin' after this thing good and proper."

He was a stout, heavy man, advanced in life. His hair was white and thick, his eyes gray. His manner was heavy and determined, like that of one accustomed to crush out, by superior mass, opposition before him. One thought of the steam roller as the man's ideal of an attacking engine.

It was night. The two were at a table in the corner of the big Waldorf dining room that looks out on Fifth Avenue. It was beyond the hour at which even the late arrival dined. It was drawing on toward midnight. A less known or a less valuable guest would hardly have kept a place in the big dining room at this hour. An old waiter hung about, evidently attached by impressive gratuities to this guest; peculiar, but with an open and enormous purse to sustain it.

The man was accustomed to obtaining what he wanted, and at any cost in money. Avarice was not a motive in the man. The motive in him, deep-seated and dominant, was power. Money was a jinn to be commanded, to fetch and carry and break open as he wished.

Arnbush and the attorney, Stetman, sat at the table after the fragments of the dinner had been removed. They were at the end of days of innumerable meetings, conferences, and legal discussions with the owners and lawyers of a business now threatened with destruction.

The great distiller chewed an unlighted cigar.

The lawyer smoked a cigarette, flicking the ashes, with care and precision, into a metal tray on the table beside his arm.

He was an able man in his profession: fertile in resources, accurate, but with a large daring that fitted him for adventuring beyond the conceptions of little counselors in the law. And he was not too elevated in his own esteem to disregard any notion of his client, however bizarre it might appear in its raw suggestion.

The distiller's big hand was thumping on the table.

"You hear what I say, Stetman! I'm goin' to land this bunch of cranks! On the day you discover the active principle in alcohol they're done! There's nothin' to it, they're done! The whole country will get drunk and stay drunk! God Almighty couldn't stop it when you get the kickdrop out of the bottle of water that's in a quart of alcohol.

"It'll take an army of agents to stop the smuggling of liquor as it is; how will they stop it if a man can carry the punch of a barrel of whisky in an ounce bottle?"

Arnbush's voice thickened with an indignant energy.

"And I'm a-goin' to put up the money to get it. I'm a-goin' to put up five millions of dollars!

"You hear what I say, Stetman! You cut out the lawsuits. This country's goin' to hell, an' I'm goin' to give it a shove along."

He extended his big hand, with a determined gesture, across the table.

"You go down to your office in the morning and write a codicil, or whatever you call it, to my will offering five millions of dollars to any chemist who discovers the active principle in alcohol."

He flung out his fat fingers.

"No ifs an' ands, Stetman, you do what I tell you!"

The lawyer very carefully removed the ashes from his cigarette. "I shall have to think about that a little," he said.

"I've already done the thinkin'," cried the distiller. "You do what I tell you!"

The explosion of his client did not disturb the lawyer. He was accustomed to this energy; and the magnitude of his fees compensated for the manner.

"It is not your intent," he said, "that I shall wish to consider; it is the form that it might take. A bald offer would hardly do. We shall have to stage the thing in some scientific purpose; perhaps a foundation of some sort would be required with your intention attached as a rider."

He paused and fingered the cigarette.

"It will be a delicate thing to handle, if one would not have the first Congress emasculate it. It may be necessary to put this fund under some other government, and to include some benefit to the arts or to the public welfare."

He paused again and one could see that he traveled in his mind, swiftly like a scouting plane, above the field of the idea. The unusual features of the thing and the obvious difficulties in the way did not drive him in upon the reply: "It cannot be done."

This was an answer he avoided. It was the secret of the man's career. To find a way, he took in every case, to be the purpose of his employment; and he climbed into a fortune on it. He held Arnbush and others of his kind because they were never met with that reply. He found a way in some sort of fashion.

Arnbush was quieted by this reflection.

"Sure!" he said. "That's what I pay you for, Stetman. You fix the thing so it'll hold water."

The lawyer continued, as though he were suggesting devices to himself:

"It might be advisable to indicate the existence of this offer to the leading chemists in the country. There is Lang and Neinsoul, just beyond us here on Park Avenue. No better man in America than Lang; fine type of Swiss. I don't know why he holds on to the German name in the firm, except that it is one of the most celebrated firm names in the world.... Great genius, Neinsoul; no doubt about it—incredible things to his name. I suppose Lang feels that the firm name is a sort of trade-mark."

The lawyer paused.

"I might see Lang on the way down—and sound him a bit; he's a late owl, usually in Keator's after midnight.... I'd like to know what a first-class chemist like Lang would think about the possibilities of a discovery of this sort.... Surely somebody has undertaken it. There must be an active principle, as you say, in alcohol—some chemical element upon which it depends for its effect. And it might be possible to separate that from the other medium. It may be, in fact, some powerful element, of which there are only slight traces in the alcohol of commercial liquors."

The big distiller thrust himself forward in his chair.

"Sure, Stetman!" he said. "Ain't our chemists been saying that all along? And ain't they been huntin' it?... But they're too little for the job! Sure, there's something in alcohol that gives it the punch."

"Well," the lawyer replied, "Lang is a pretty big man.... I'll see you in the morning."

He rose. Arnbush went out with him into the corridor and, when the lawyer had gone, he took the elevator to his room.

But Arnbush did not go at once to bed. He sat down by the window, looking out on the avenue and the passing vehicles, and through the cañons and vistas of the city, blue in the starlit night.

He was bitter and determined.

The great business of which he was the leading spirit had been ruined. He saw clearly that this was the end. He had a larger vision and a sounder judgment than his associates. Their desperate legal writhings almost amused him. They were plainly useless.

Revenge was the only consolation open.

He had an immense fortune, an incredible fortune; well, he would use a portion of it to nullify the victory of his enemies. He would sow their hopes with ruin, such ruin as the half-mad creatures never imagined. They could regulate and limit the use of commercial liquor, but the thing he would discover they could neither control nor regulate. Like Samson he would lay hold of the pillars of the house and all should go down to ruin with him. He would offer a sum so great that the ablest chemists of the world would be in his service. Five millions of dollars should go into this discomfiture of his enemies.

He sat a long time before the window; finally a sound disturbed him. The telephone bell was ringing. He rose and went over to it. The voice speaking seemed far away, and the man thought it was a long-distance call from some remote point.

"This is Neinsoul," the voice said. "Come to our laboratory on Park Avenue; I think we have discovered the thing you are looking for."

It was a moment before Arnbush realized the message. Evidently Stetman had seen his man. And the chemists were keen; their interest could not wait. Well, five millions was a huge sum. They might very well fear that a cooler mood in the rich distiller would reduce the offer. But the hour was late, and Arnbush replied with some urgency upon the point.

The thin, distant voice was insistent.

"I shall not be here in the morning; you must come to-night."

This repeated answer seemed final and decisive. In the course of an ordinary affair Arnbush would have ordered the speaker to remain and await his arrival in the morning. But the voice seemed one not easily to be ordered. And Arnbush was still hot with the moving impulses of his affair. There was no mood for sleep on him, although the night was advanced. And he determined to go. He got his coat and hat and descended into the street.

A few minutes brought him to the number.

The building, gaunt with its lightless windows, was abandoned. But the door to the dark entrance opened as he approached.

"We shall have to walk up," a voice said. "It is not far."

Arnbush could not see the man; but he recognized the voice, and he went in. It seemed a long journey up the stairs. Finally they came into a room lighted dimly, above a table, with a gas jet.

The room was fitted with all the devices of a chemist's trade; there was the faint, pungent odor of such a place about it. Two tall windows looked out above the city, and there was a chair and a stool beside the table.

The chemist was now visible to Arnbush: a tall, stooped figure in a sort of smock; a big, nearly naked head, bulging above the brows and fringed with straw-colored hair; a pasty face, livid and unhealthy; and thick, myopic glasses that reduced the eyes behind them.

The chemist took the stool behind the table and indicated the chair before it for his guest.

Arnbush was fatigued with the long climb, and he at once sat down.

The chemist came directly to the point; he made no disquisition on his wealthy patron, the hour, or the affair.

"I have discovered the thing you are seeking," he said. "I will show it to you."

He took a little glass tube from a rack before him and held it under the light. It was partly filled with a thick, viscous, golden-colored stuff.

"That is circine," he said. "It is the element of virtue in all distillations. In alcohol," he continued, "one finds it imperfectly produced. This sample I am showing you is pure."

He rose, got a glass, filled it halfway with water from a spigot, added a drop of the fluid from the tube and handed it to Arnbush.

"Drink that," he said.

The golden-colored essence had disappeared completely into the water, making a rich amber liquid, and the man thought that he was about to taste something peculiar or unpleasant.

He got the staggering shake-up of his life.

At the first touch of the liquid to his tongue, the man paused, removed the glass, and sat back in his chair, looking in wonder at the chemist.

He had tasted something heavenly! The aroma of a soft, aged, velvety liquor was in his mouth; a liquor beyond the product of any human distillation; the liquor that one has dreamed of, forgotten in some ancient cask, bedded down in cobwebs in a warehouse, or hidden by one's father through a lifetime.

The man was too shaken to be coherent. He began to stutter.

The chemist was undisturbed.

"Drink it," he said.

Arnbush leaned over and drank off the fluid, And at once every sensation in his body changed: a warm glow extended to his fingers; there was soft, insidious stimulation, and the fatigue of his exertions vanished.

And there was more than this.

The ego in the man was elevated. It took on dominance and majesty; bothered and hectored, heretofore, it was now a king. And the spirit of the man, rising as though newly born in some womb of the sun, realized that this was the thing that every human creature tasting of liquors eternally longed for. It was the thing for which the world had been going to alcohol to seek—the supreme, moving motive of all drunkenness! It released, and strengthened, and ennobled that thing within the human body which every man thinks of as himself.

Or at least it seemed like that to Arnbush.

And there was with this heavenly taste of liquor the alluring enchantment of a drug. The world softened and became a place of pleasure, but it was the pleasure of a mental dominance, and it was the softness of a plastic kingdom. The individuality in the man was glorified.

What alcohol promised, this amazing fluid gave!

Arnbush put down the empty glass, and regarded the chemist, across the table, with a growing wonder.

"You have found it!" he said.

It was the comment of one who finds a treasure; the comment of one who, after a doubtful search, looks down on a heap of gold-pieces gleaming under the broken lid-boards of a chest.

"You have found it!"

It was the supreme expression of a victory immense and final. He had now within his hand the ruin of his enemies. And the stimulated ego in the man exulted. He would destroy their victory over him beyond the wildest conceptions of disaster. They were now trapped and huddled, and the weapon was in his hand.

His revenge stood out a shining figure before his face!

No need now for the trust fund in a death testament. He should live to see it. And he put the eager query, foremost in his mind.

"Is it difficult to manufacture?"

The chemist had been sitting with his elbow on the table, his jaw bedded in the fork of his hand, his pale eyes behind the myopic lenses on Arnbush.

It was a strange reflective watching, as of one who was beyond the common motives of a normal life; as of one who sat at a window, before a world that it no longer interested him to enter, or out of which he had been ejected—and who, being thus, had found a medium for vicarious influence.

He replied without a change in his peculiar posture.

"It is the widest distributed of all known elements," he said, "and the easiest to isolate.... Anybody can make it and the material is before every door. I bid you observe how simple the process is."

He removed his hand, drew forth a drawer in the table and took out a candle, an ordinary clay pipe and some green, little seed. He packed the seed into the pipe bowl with his thumb and set it above the flame.

Arnbush looked on, astonished.

The temperature of the night had changed. A faint premonition of the morning was on the way. There was a suggestion of chill entering through the window. And there was silence.

The dim flame of the gas jet overhead and the candle on the table threw a flickering arc of light about the pale hand, the clay pipe with its bowl of seed sitting in the flame, and the big, nearly naked, head extended toward them.

And while the distiller watched, there appeared, at the mouth end of the pipe stem, a drop of green. It lengthened and widened slowly until it hung there like a pear-shaped emerald.

The chemist removed the pipe from the flame of the candle.

"That is circine," he said. "It is present in all vegetable life, especially in the seed. Any of the plants of the Ambrosia family are rich in it. I have used here the common green seed of the ragweed and a little heat.

"But I bid you mark that in this form the circine is not free. It is locked up in the molecule. If you tasted this drop of green, it would be bitter and have no effect. The circine is, as I have said, cased off in the molecule. It must be freed to have any virtue."

He rose, got a broken-handled cup and from a plate beside it a pinch of substance that looked like a gray mold, pulverized it between his fingers, placed it in the cup, and added the drop of green liquid on the pipe stem.

He warmed the cup above the candle, and presently, when he had finished, handed it to Arnbush.

Within lay a globule of the golden fluid!

"Here," he said, "we have the circine free. Taste it."

He took the cup and added a little water.

The distiller touched it to his lips, and with a great effort of the will replaced it on the table. In his mouth was, again, the taste of that rich, heavenly liquor, seasoned, an age long, in some hidden cask.

The chemist went back to his stool.

"The substance I have added to the drop of green is a fungus culture. Among the innumerable varieties of fungi there is, alone, one culture which has the power to destroy the shell about the molecule and set the incased circine free. And as it happens, this fungus is of almost universal distribution; is as available as bread mold."

He paused, and added:

"As I have said, circine is the very commonest of all elements, and the simplest to obtain. A workman can make it with his pipe, adding a pinch of this fungus—as I have shown you with these humble implements."

The chemist paused and resumed his posture, his chin gathered into his hand; his eyes, diminished by the thick lenses, on Arnbush, in that reflective watching as of one looking from a window.

And the distiller saw, in a vast sweep of vision, the effect of this discovery.

As by the rubbing of a lamp he had obtained the thing he wished for, more perfectly adapted than his wish could hope. From this day the whole world would be drunken. No human creature, having tasted of this heavenly liquor, would return to abstinence; no laws could possibly prevent its use. A thing that any man could make with a clay pipe, some seeds, and a pinch of fungus was beyond a sumptuary law. Once known, even a death sentence on the thing would be a dead letter in a statute.

And the man thrilled, in a great upward sweep of the heart, at this ruin of his enemies.

He saw what he would do. He would hold the secret, buy advertising space in every newspaper, and on a given day make the whole thing known. Once the discovery was known, he saw clearly, not even the infinity of God could prevent a drunken world.

Arnbush rose and went over to the window. The city lay dumb and silent before him. His enemies were sleeping in their beds, and he stood above them, with their ruin in his hand.

It was a great, expanded moment.

Arnbush remained with his hands behind him, looking out. There was no sound or evidence of life behind him. When, finally, he turned, the chemist was sitting in that watchful pose.

The distiller spoke, in the vigor of his victory.

"This is the greatest thing that was ever discovered!"

Neinsoul replied without moving, without a gesture.

"We consider circine," he said, "the most important element so far re-leased by us. The habit-forming drugs upon which we have heretofore de-pended are limited in their influence, and we have obtained from them only a fragmentary result. We have long sought something of universal appeal."

"Well, you got it," interrupted Arnbush; "the country'll drink itself into hell on this stuff."

In his satisfaction he overlooked the chemist's plural pronoun.

The muscles about Neinsoul's lips distended in a sort of weird smile.

"We shall hardly hope for that," he said. "In fact, the effect of circine on the human body is not deleterious. Neither depression nor nausea fol-lows its use; there are none of the unpleasant after-effects of alcohol, or the so-called habit-forming drugs. In truth, many persons of weak individuality will be physically advanced by circine."

He continued to speak distinctly, in his thin, distant voice.

"It is the prime virtue in circine that it builds up and hardens the indi-viduality of the user. It makes him, in the end, wholly self-sufficient. He will not go to another for any element of sensation. It is the influence of exterior organisms that the circine continually resists.

"All drugs released by us have had some psychic effect, as for example, the degenerative moral effect of opium. This psychic influence of circine is not degenerative in the individual, but it is eliminative of all influences psychic, exterior to the individual. I do not mean that it touches ordinary sensation which is of physical origin. But it removes all response to foreign psychic stimuli or physical stimuli moving from a psychic origin—as, for example, the love lure in its various psychic and psycho-physical expres-sions.

"Under the influence of circine, that basic element of the individual which he calls himself is built up to a completeness which will wholly re-ject any sensation depending upon another, whether that sensation be psy-chic, as in morals, or psycho-physical, as in the love lure."

He paused abruptly, and looked up. The air entering through the win-dow was beginning to freshen; a faint gray haze was appearing in the sky behind the city. And the chemist acted like one in haste to an appointment. He seized a tablet, in the drawer before him, tore off a sheet, wrote hastily upon it, and thrust it across the table to Arnbush.

"There is the chemical formula of circine," he said, "and the name of the fungus. I must go."

The distiller began to speak about his offer, the lawyer Stetman, the other partner, Lang, and what should now be done in payment and the legal transfer.

But the chemist hurried him; he could not listen; he had no time, and it was unimportant.

In some confusion and as swiftly as he could, Arnbush descended the stair and went out into the street. The door clicked behind him, and he heard the footsteps of the chemist going down as though to pass out through the basement.

Morning had now arrived. And Arnbush returned across the city to the Waldorf.

But he returned like one entering with a triumph. He walked, his shoulders thrown back, his head up, like a conquerer. The effect of this wondrous fluid, even from his taste of it, remained. He would impose his will on this crank-ridden country, and he had the power folded in his pocket.

He began to go over in his mind the things Neinsoul had said.

He had some knowledge of the phraseology of such a trade, from the chemists employed about his manufactories; and he understood the substance of the discourse. He reviewed it now carefully in detail. This stuff was circine. It was the active principle in all fermentation; one got it from green seed, heat, and a pinch of fungus. And he passed on into a scrutiny of Neinsoul's statement about the effect of circine.

He was in this abstraction when, at the entrance to the hostelry, he stopped.

There was some bustle about the door. A limousine stood open and a young man and a girl were getting out. There was rice scattered on its fenders; and the two were radiant. Their manner was infectious; passers stopped, the hall boys and the porters had come out—all were smiling.

Arnbush followed them inside.

He drew near to the young man and the girl, and he observed them closely. It was no new incident in the common life. But before the formula he carried in his pocket the scene had a peculiar interest.

It was scheduled in his plan to cease.

He marked the power, the stimulus, the resistless charm of this thing Neinsoul had called the love lure. The hardest creature about his task paused and stood up smiling, as though the incident released within him some memory or some hope.

Arnbush walked about, thrusting through the group of persons, to keep the two within the sweep of his eye. He would miss no detail. And when they passed out of his sight and hearing he stood for some time looking at the elevator as at the abandoned spot of some transfiguration.

Then he filled his big lungs and shrugged his shoulders. Well, there would be no more of this thing! And he went in to breakfast.

The old waiter was slow this morning and, Arnbush thought, inattentive. He spoke to him sharply.

The man was obsequious and apologetic. His wife was ill; he was in acute distress. They had been long together, and happy; dependent on each other; the twain one flesh, as the mystic words expressed it.... If she should die!

Arnbush plunged his hand into his pocket, drew out his purse and gave the man a bill. It was in three figures. But the distiller was accustomed to add substance to his sympathy—not words only, although the words were from the heart.

"There, there, Henry! She'll pull through." And he patted the old man on the shoulder.

This was impulse. Upon reflection he moved a little in the chair.

The memory of Neinsoul watching as from a window occurred to him.

He drank a little coffee and got up. But he could find no cigar to suit him. He tried a handful and threw them down. He wandered awhile about the corridors and finally went out. He would walk down to Stetman's office. It was early, but the lawyer was accustomed to come in early, in order to be undisturbed at his morning's work.

The air had come in from the sea; it was fresh and vital, and as the man walked he began to recover some measure of his poise. Several blocks down Fifth Avenue, he stopped.

A procession of small children in some religious ceremony was coming up on the other side. He waited until they were opposite; then he crossed. He walked slowly along the line, paused, and, returning, passed it again. He looked with a profound, a consuming, an eager interest at each child.

He watched the procession disappear, took a step or two, and then, hurrying to the curb, began to gesticulate wildly with his stick. A taxicab answered; he plunged in and shouted an address.

Stetman was among his law books when his client entered. He rose from his stooped posture.

"I was working on your matter," he said.

Arnbush came forward, shouting from the threshold:

"Well! You don't have to work on it no longer. I got it. Do you see that, Stetman? Do you see what's on that paper?"

He thrust Neinsoul's formula before the astonished lawyer. The man looked at the chemical hieroglyphics and the text below it, written in a fine, accurate, thin hand.

"Where did you get this?" he said.

"Where did I get it!" cried the distiller. "You know where I got it. I got it from your firm of chemists, Lang and Neinsoul."

The lawyer stepped back from his table.

"I didn't see Lang," he said, "he was not at Keator's."

Arnbush went on shouting in his excitement.

"Anyhow, I got it of Neinsoul! An' you see what I'm goin' to do with it!"

He flourished the paper a moment, wildly, before the lawyer's strange, contracted face, and then he tore it into bits, scattering the fragments about the room.

And, oblivious to the amazement in Stetman, he went on shouting. The very act of tearing the formula seemed to increase the fury of his manner.

"You think I'm crazy, eh! Well, I ain't crazy! What for do I want to stop a young feller from falling in love with his sweetheart?... What for do I want to break up the companionship of old people?... What for do I want to keep all the little children out of the world?... You hear what I say, Stetman?"

The lawyer thought his client was insane. He came around the table, his face drawn.

"Who have you seen?" he said.

Arnbush was now in a fury of declamation.

"Neinsoul!" he shouted. "Ain't I told you! ... Neinsoul! He called me up on the telephone after you left. An' I went over to their laboratory on Park Avenue."

"And Neinsoul was there?"

The lawyer's voice was low, tense, amazed.

"Sure, he was there," Arnbush roared. "Ain't I told you!"

The lawyer made a single exclamation.

"Good God!" he said.

Arnbush turned on him, swinging heavily on his big feet, as on some ponderous hinges.

"What for do you say, 'Good God'?"

"Because," replied the lawyer, "if Neinsoul was there, he got out of hell to come.... He died three years ago in Essen, poisoned by a blinding gas that he had invented for the German army."

CHAPTER XIII

THE SYMBOL

To Marion Dillard there was mockery in the symbolism of the night.

She was alone. On the table before her was an open telegram—the grating fitted into the last opening of the trap. She was a dark-haired, slender girl with that aspect of capacity and independence with which the great war endowed our women: the high courage that no assault of evil fortune could bludgeon into servility. She sat in her chair before the table, to the eye, unconquered.

But it was to the eye only. In the magnificence about her the wreckage impending was incredible; the great house fitted with every luxury, the library in which she sat, its rug the treasure of a temple, its walls paneled!

To Marion Dillard, in her chair before the table, with the telegram open before her, the whole setting was grotesque. All over the city, white with newly fallen snow, were the symbols of this majestic celebration of the birth of the Saviour. They were not absent in this room. Holly wreaths hung in the windows, and the strange ivory image, representing the crucifixion of Jesus of Nazareth, which her father had always so greatly prized, had been brought out, after the usual custom on this night, and placed on the table. It sat on a black silk cloth embroidered with a white cross. As a work of art it was not conspicuously excellent; but her father prized it for the memory of a great adventure.

Marion Dillard leaned back in the chair, reviewing the events that had moved against her as though with some sinister design. Her father was dead. A cross of white marble stood on a hilltop in France to his memory. It had been erected by every people in the great war, for her father, moved by a high, adventurous idealism, too old for longer service in the American army, had taken his own fortune—and, alas, the fortune which he held in trust for another—and with it maintained a hospital base on the western front for the benefit of every injured man, friend or enemy.

Marion Dillard reflected: Of what avail was it that her father had not realized that this trust money was going into his big conception? He had drawn on his resources in America until every item of his great fortune was pledged, and by some error, this estate, in trust, had gone into the common fund. Appalled, when she came to examine the accounts, Marion had endeavored to cover the matter, hoping that the decision of the United States Circuit Court of Appeals in a suit to recover a tract of coal lands in the south would be decided in favor of her father's estate, and thus furnish the money to replace this trust. And so she had somehow managed to go on.

This telegram on the table was the end. "Reversed and dismissed," were the sinister words of it. On this night commemorating the birth of that great founder of brotherhood, whose idealistic conceptions her father had always so magnificently followed, she must decide what she would do.

The thing was sharp and clear before her. She must either wreck the majestic legend of her father, or degrade herself! As she had carried the thing along by various shifts since her father's death, she could easily make it appear that she had, herself, embezzled this trust fund. That would leave the memory of her father clean; but it clearly meant that she herself could not escape the criminal courts. The heirs of her father's friend were insistent and hostile. They would have the pound of flesh, now that the fortune was gone.

For a time she sat motionless, her eyes vaguely on the carved ivory image on the table before her. Then, she got up, and, with her hands clasped behind her back, stood looking down at the crucifix.

It was about ten inches high, rudely carved in the Chinese fashion out of the segment of an elephant's tusk four inches in diameter. The cross represented the trunk of a tree, the roots thrust out for the base. The figure, with arms extended, was nailed to the broken limbs of this tree-trunk, forming the cross. The whole top of the tree-trunk made the head of the figure, thrown back under a crown of thorns. And there in the quaint English letters cut around the base was the legend: "Inasmuch as you have turned your head to save us, may He turn His head to save you."

Well, the thing was an idle hope. There was no help in the world: either her own life or the memory of her father was on the way to dreadful wreckage!

Then desperation overcame her. She went out of the library through the great hall to the door. A maid helped her into her coat. She gave a direction that the servants should be dismissed for the night, no one should remain up, she would let herself in with her latchkey when she returned. She went out.

At the bronze gates as she passed into the street a man sauntering along the wall spoke to her. She knew him at once. It was Walker of the Secret Service. So they were already beginning to keep her under surveillance! The explanation of this detective did not mislead her. He was looking for a dangerous criminal, he said, who had come into the city and had made inquiries about this house.

Marion Dillard replied with some polite appreciation of the thoughtfulness of the police for her security, and went on. At the end of the bronze fence, as she passed, she observed another figure crouched against the wall as though it also kept guard on her house; but it moved away as she approached, as though to conceal itself around the turn of the wall inclosing the spacious grounds. She smiled grimly. The watch kept on her would be efficient; here was another. She went along the street to the great bridge.

She paused for a moment before the immense stone lions on their great pedestals at the bridge head. They looked old, haggard, changing into monsters under a draping of snow! Then she set out to walk across the bridge into the country beyond, past the cathedral on the hill, lighted, and from which the melody of vague and distant music descended. And the feeling in the girl as she moved dreadfully in the night, became a sort of wonder. Was this a vast delusion, or was there in fact a Will in the universe determined on righteousness, and moving events to the aid of those who devoted their lives to its service?

She went on, walking stiffly like a dead body hypnotized into a pretension of life.

* * * *

There was no sound on the sea. It was a vast, endless desert of water on which the sun lay as though fixed. Only the chugging of the rusted freighter broke the immobility of the silence. The tramp looked like a battered derelict, not battered by the stormy elements of the sea; but haggard by the creeping detritus of inactivities in crowded tropical ports. The steel hull was covered with rust; the stack leprous, and the metal devices of the deck newly covered with a cheap paint.

There was no breath of air in the world, either to disturb the immense placidity of the sea or to vary the thin line of smoke vaguely blending into the distant sky line.

Two men sat against a drum on the rear of the ship. If one had been searching the world for types of the worst human derelicts, the search would have ended at the drum on the rear of this tramp. The types were villainous, but they were distinct—in marked contrast. The little man was speaking.

"Cut along with it, Colonel," he said. "How much did the Chink give you?"

He was a thin, nervous creature, with a habit of fingering his face, as though to remove some invisible thing clinging to it. It was impossible to place the man, either in nationality or environment of life. He might have been a Cockney, born under the Bow Bells; but it was more probable that he was a New York gunman. He had picked up habits of speech in every degraded port of the east, as a traveling rat picks up a scurvy.

The man he addressed was big, with a putty-colored face, dead-black hair plastered down with water over an immense head beginning to grow bald. He was dressed in a worn frock coat—the clothes of a clergyman—threadbare, but clean. His shoes, even, showed evidences of an attempt at polish. He wore a clean, white, starched shirt and a low collar with a black string tie. A huge black stogy hung in the corner of his mouth. He sat relaxed in a heap against the drum, he had a white handkerchief over his shirt front, tucked into the collar in order to protect his linen from the ash and while his body remained immobile he whittled a piece of pine board. The long knife blade polished to the edge of a razor, moved on the wood as in some grotesque manner of caress. He gave the appearance of one unutterably weary; an immense sagging body in which all the fibers were relaxed.

He was devitalized with opium.

His voice, when he spoke, presented the same evidence of utter languor. His lips scarcely moved, and the sound seemed to creep out in a slow drawl.

"The Chink gave me two yellow boys. He had six in his hand. 'You bring Major Dillard of the American Division here to-night,' he said, 'and you get the other four.' Of course, he didn't speak English. He spoke the Manchu dialect. I know the Manchu dialect. That's where I had a flock; but I came in when the Boxers started. That's how I came to be on hand when the Allied armies began their march under old von Waldersee.... You understand, I had left the mission."

He spoke with a nice discriminating care in the selection of his words, as though it were a thing in which he had a particular and consuming pride. The gunman laughed.

"You mean you had been kicked to hell out of it, and were livin' on the country."

There was a faint protest in the Colonel's drawl.

"It's true I was not sent out by any of the great sectarian missions. I adopted the work, and I was not in favor with the regular organizations in China. They resisted my endeavors."

"I'd say they did," his companion interrupted. "You're the worst crook in the world barrin' one, not so far away." He laughed. "There's a circular posted up in every mission in Asia givin' your mug, and tellin' what a damned impostor you are. Some vitriol in the descriptions of you, Colonel. I've seen 'em."

The man was not disturbed. The drawl continued:

"Yes, Mr. Bow Bell," he said; "quite true, quite true. I was not in favor with the regular organizations."

The names which the two derelicts applied to one another they had themselves selected, inspired by the impression produced upon each other at the time of their meeting on the ship. The big man had called the gunman Mr. Bow Bell, and the gunman had named his companion Colonel Swank. They had made no further inquiry. Men of this character are not concerned about names.

Bow Bell put his fingers over his face, drawing them gently down and removing them together from the point of his chin, as though he brushed something away.

"So you crawled out of your rat hole, when the column started, to see what you could pinch. Good pickin', eh, what?"

Colonel Swank made a low, murmured exclamation.

"History tells us," he said, "how the rich cities of antiquity were looted by the soldiery of invading armies; but there can hardly have been a parallel to this in any known case. The whole country for a considerable distance on either side of the line of march was denuded of every article of value, even the venerated images of Buddha in the holy temple of Ten Thousand Ages were broken to pieces with dynamite, under the impression that they concealed articles of value. Of course, the Chinese population stowed away everything they could; but they could not hide the women, and they were not always able to conceal their treasures; such as carved ivory, cloisonné, vases, silks, furs, and the like."

"The lid was off," said Bow Bell, "about as it would be in India if the English went out. I once asked a Rajah in the Punjab what he would do if the English left India, and you ought to have seen his grin. 'I'd take my regiment and go down to the coast, and there wouldn't be a virgin or a ten-anna bit left in Bombay.' ... Cut along with your story. The Chink gave you two gold twenties to bring in Major Dillard, with four more in his hand if you put it over. You brought him in, didn't you? Gawd, is there anything you wouldn't do for a hundred and twenty dollars! Name it, Colonel, let me hear what it sounds like."

Swank's voice did not change. He was unresponsive to the taunt.

"Yes," he said, "I was so fortunate as to induce Major Dillard to visit the monastery under my guidance, though it required some diplomatic effort, and some insistence; but the Major had confidence in my cloth, and he was making every effort to prevent a looting of the country along the line of march."

Bow Bell laughed in a high staccato.

"Confidence in your cloth! It was just a piece of your damned luck that the American officer never heard of you. He thought you were an honest-to-God missionary. You'd know all the tricks. You'd be sanctimonious enough to fool the Devil, for a handful of yellow boys minted in America. I'd lay a quid on the Saints that you fooled him all right.... Well, go on and tell me about it. You say the old Viceroy, with the Boxers on one side and the foreign devils on the other, was cooped up in a monastery along the line of march, with the women of all the important families in the Province, and everything of value that they hadn't time to bury. You'd nose it out, Johnny-on-the-spot. You couldn't get it yourself—some Chink would have put a knife in you—and it was no good to you for the foreign devils to get it, so you took your little old hundred and twenty, and went in to the American Headquarters to see Major Dillard, eh, what!"

He went on condensing the unessentials in the hope of getting Colonel Swank forward with his narrative.

"The viceroy was sick, and too old to travel. It was all he could do to sit up. His only chance was to put himself under the protection of the American Expeditionary Force. The English were on ahead, and he knew what the Russians and Germans would do to him. Gawd! He'd gathered it up for 'em! It was like saying, 'Come along, boys. I've got the stuff corralled for you. Here's the girlies, and here's the pieces of eight. Go to it. Gawd!... No wonder they dug up the yellow boys.... You'd 'a' got more if you had held out. Did that occur to you?"

Swank made a vague gesture,—a languorous moving of his hand over his threadbare knee.

"One should not consider a reward for aiding others in distress; besides my resources were very low at the time, and American gold in the East was at a premium."

"Too hungry to trade, eh, what?" said Bow Bell. "I have been like that; but you must have been damned hungry, Colonel. Gawd! You must have been starved to the bone ... cut along. Was it night?"

"It was evening," continued Colonel Swank. "Night was coming on by the time I had persuaded Major Dillard to come with me. I had a good deal of difficulty to get him to come with me alone, without a guard. Not that he was afraid. This American officer was not afraid. You could tell that by his face. There was no way to frighten him; but it was irregular, and he had practically to go incognito. The Viceroy had stipulated with me that I should bring the American officer alone. He did not wish the common soldiers to know what the monastery contained. I had some difficulty to convince Major Dillard; but as I have said, he had faith in my cloth."

"Gawd," said the gunman, and he spat violently on the deck. "Suppose he had been on to you, you damned old renegade. My word, you were in luck!... Did they send a yellow chair?"

The placidity of Swank was unmoved.

"No," he said, "as it happened, the chairs were red. It was some of the chairs in which the women had been brought in. You know, a bride in China is always sent to the house of her husband in a red chair. All the red chairs in the province had been commandeered to bring in the young daughters of the high Chinese residents, to the protection of the Viceroy. They sent what they had. Yellow is the Royal color in China. The Viceroy couldn't use it."

Bow Bell interrupted with a sort of vehemence.

"Damn it, man, get on. You're the slowest brute I ever saw to get into a story. It was night when you set out with Major Dillard in the red chairs. How far was it to the monastery?"

But the deliberation of Swank's narration was not to be hurried. His hand moved the long sharp blade of his knife slowly along the piece of soft wood, removing a shaving like a ribbon. He went on in his slow drawl.

"The monastery was a few miles west of the advancing column. The American Division had just come up; behind it was a smart regiment from Berlin; and behind that, farther down, were the Russians. You see the whole Expeditionary Force in China had been put under the command of Count von Waldersee. The German Emperor had intrigued for this supreme command; had, in fact, openly solicited it from the Chancelleries of Europe. You will find it all described in the memoirs of von Eckerman. The German Emperor thought he would make a great point in the world if the supreme command of the allied forces in China should be put under a German officer. The Asiatic would be impressed with the superior importance of German Arms—'Observe, if you please, how all Nations looking about for a leader have selected a German general!'"

Swank paused as from the weariness of effort.

"The Emperor was immensely keen about it; but it only made the Chancelleries of Europe laugh. It was Wilhelm II at his theatricals; besides, any Prime Minister of discretion could see the awkward situations that would confront the nominal head of the Expeditionary Forces; and so the Chancelleries of Europe laughed, and, turning away their faces, gravely acceded to the Emperor's request. That is how von Waldersee came to command the column. He was a big, purple-faced German, wearing a helmet with a black eagle on the top of it, and a white chin strap; and he always rode a black charger. The theatrical conceptions of the Emperor must be carried out in detail. And the officious von Waldersee was overlooking no occasion. An orderly had just arrived from the German High Command as I entered to interview Major Dillard, and as it happened the American general put the message, that this orderly carried, into his pocket as he came out with me."

Bow Bell cursed under his breath.

"I know all that," he said. "Everybody knows it. Get on to the real thing. What happened to the Viceroy, and the girlies, and the loot?"

Undisturbed, unmoved, and deliberate, Colonel Swank continued with his narrative.

"We set out in the red chairs. I was in front, for I was to lead the way, and Major Dillard was directly behind. We traveled for about three miles west, across the fields, and then through a wood to a slight elevation on which the monastery was situated. We passed first under that queer thing which is to be found in China—a sort of gateway, and triumphal arch; but without any supporting wall about it. This arch had now a big tarpaulin stretched across it on which was painted an immense white cross. Through the arch, on a flag-paved road we approached the main structure of the monastery. True to the usual form of architecture, the lower part was of stone, and the upper part of wood. It was crowned by towers, roofed with yellow tiles, and painted in vivid colors. On the corner of the roof were innumerable bells, that rang weirdly in the slight wind. On either side of it, standing on immense pedestals were two enormous lions. Very strange these lions appeared before us as we entered the paved court. They had that old haggard, sinister aspect that the Oriental alone can give to the features of a beast; that aspect of merging, as by some degeneration, into a monster. Before us was a double-roofed square tower, with a door on either side.

"We got down from the chairs and went in. At the door stood the old Chinese official who had given me the two yellow boys. He now handed me the remaining four, and we entered the monastery. Within there was an immense image of Buddha, covered with gold leaf. The temple was lofty, and dimly lighted, and the colossal image of Buddha, glittering as though of pure gold, and holding the sacred lotus in his hand, ascended into the lofty upper spaces of the temple. A circular stairway, mounted around the inner walls of the temple so that one might go up to the very face of the Buddha, sitting in his eternal calm.

"All along this stairway there were images in clay, painted in divers colors.

"About us as we entered the temple were crowds of Buddhist priests, their heads shaven, and wearing the characteristic dress—the long yellow robe confined at the waist by a sash, and felt-soled slippers. They moved noiselessly, as though they were the spirit company attendant on this immense image. However, we were not come to idle before the wonders of a Buddhist monastery. The Chinese official went on and we followed behind him. He passed through a door at the rear of the shrine, and we were at once in an immense, low room. It was a very big room.

"One was not able to see what decorations the walls had contained, as they were heaped on all sides to the ceiling with bales of silks, furs, and embroideries; and all about were chests and boxes, piled in some confusion, as though they had just been brought in. The whole chamber was a warehouse, and it was filled to the ceiling, except for a narrow passage through the middle. This we traversed, and, coming to the end of it, passed through a yellow door into another chamber. We entered here a room of lesser dimensions; but it was fitted up after the usual idea of Chinese luxury—great mirrors around the walls; rich rugs on the floor; a variety of clocks, all going at a different hour; and many screens and tapestries.

"In the middle of the room in a chair padded with silk cushions sat the Viceroy. He was an ancient man, evidently at the end of life. His face was like wrinkled parchment. The white, straggling beard remained on his face; but the whole dome of his skull was bald. It was as bare as the palm of a hand. It was yellow with age.

"But the most striking thing in the place was the women.

"The whole room was literally crowded with young Chinese women; the daughters of the important men of the province. They sat about on the priceless carpets, clothed in exquisite silks, embroidered with designs of their hereditary houses. They looked like quaint dolls, their hair knotted in the usual Chinese fashion with gum, and thrust through with ornaments of jade, and gold pins; their mouths painted."

"Gawd," said Bow Bell, "what a layout for the Hun! Mohammed couldn't beat it in his heaven. Get along!"

Colonel Swank continued in his dreary, monotonous voice.

"The Viceroy was too ill to rise; but he made a salute in the German fashion with his hand when Major Dillard entered; and he began at once to address the American through the Chinese official who accompanied us, and whose English was as good as my own. He asked for protection to the Monastery, and a guard; and extending his hand to the great storeroom through which we had passed, he offered the American anything that he wished in payment for this protection. Major Dillard endeavored to explain that the Allied Armies were not on a quest of loot; but were merely endeavoring to relieve the legations at Pekin, and establish order in the country; that they could receive no compensation for this service; and that he would endeavor to protect the Monastery.

"But he was disturbed about a guard.

"The American Expeditionary Force was not large, and he was easily able to see the international complications that might arise if he left here an American guard to clash, perhaps, with the German division behind him."

Swank moved slightly in his position against the drum of the freighter. The ash from the half-burned stogy fell on the white cotton handkerchief. There came a shadow of interest into his voice.

"At this moment," he said, "while Major Dillard was engaged with the difficult problem before him, an extraordinary event occurred. There was a clamor of voices outside. A Chinese guard hurtled through the door, and fell on the floor before the Viceroy. There was a sound of heavy footsteps, the clang of side arms, the echo of guttural voices, and a moment later a dozen German officers entered the room.

"They were young Prussian under-officers from the portion of the German company behind the American Division. They stopped inside the door, lost for a moment in wonder at the very miracle of the thing they were seeking. Then they noticed Major Dillard standing beside the Viceroy's chair. They brought their heels together and made him a formal military salute; but it was clear they regarded him as of no particular importance—as merely a soldier from the American Division to be accorded the usual amenities; but not to be permitted to interfere with any design they had in mind.

"There followed a brief, verbal passage at arms, with a shattering dramatic sequel.

"Major Dillard explained that the Monastery was under the protection of the American Division; that it must not be disturbed; and requested the German officers to withdraw. They replied with a courtesy in which there was a high contempt; that as the American Division had passed on, and the German Company arrived on the ground, the Monastery was under the *protection*—they got a sneering, contemptuous note in the word—of the German Expeditionary Force, and they must insist on their right of control.

"They looked about at the rich loot, the ancient Viceroy, and the painted women, and what they meant by protection to the monastery was as clear as light.

"They were all under the influence of liquor; one or two of them were plainly drunk. It was evident that Major Dillard could not control them, and it was clear that their contention of their right of control over the Chinese territory adjacent to their Division was in point of legal virtue superior to that of the American Division that had passed on, and from which Major Dillard had returned here. They spoke with an exaggerated courtesy to the American; but they were clearly intending to seize the monastery, to ignore any claim of the Americans over it, and they made that intention insolently evident. The old Chinese Viceroy understood it at once. Despair enveloped him. His chin dropped on his bosom, and he put out his hands like one resigned to the inevitable. The young, insolent Prussians advanced into the room.

"It was at this moment that the dramatic sequel arrived."

Colonel Swank paused; he made a slight gesture with the hand in which the long sharp blade of his knife moved on the soft wood.

"I have mentioned," he said, "how in character were the acts of Wilhelm II in this international affair, and now one of these theatrical gestures intervened with a shattering dénouement. Major Dillard offered no further argument. He took out of his pocket the message which he had received from von Waldersee as we were setting out and read it: It was an order of the High Command putting a portion of a German Company under the command of that foreign general whose division it followed. And, thus, this order put the German advance guard, of which these Prussians were officers under the command of the American General. It was the Emperor's gracious return for the grant of the supreme command to von Waldersee. Major Dillard made no comment. He gave a curt order as though he were addressing a sergeant's squad:

"The Prussians were to remain and guard the Monastery during the whole of the Allied occupation; nothing should be disturbed; they would be held responsible for every life and every article, and for the rigid preservation of order. It was a hard, clear, comprehensive direction: And they were to report to him in Pekin.

"The amazement of the young Prussian officers was beyond any word to express. Their jaws dropped; their very eyes bulged. The drunken ones were instantly sober. They recognized the black eagle and the signature of the German High Command. Every vestige of human initiative vanished out of them. Von Waldersee's order was an ukase of the All Highest—the direction of the Emperor—a command of the War Lord. They formed in a line before the American, clicked their heels, and saluted. And he set them about the outside of the Monastery as a guard; and went away in his chair."

Bow Bell threw himself forward from the iron drum of the tramp with a great cackle of laughter.

"Gawd!" he cried. "Could you beat it! A look-in, and then to be snapped up like that! Gawd!" He rocked himself on the deck, his hands clasped about his knees. "I can see 'em," he stuttered. "Oh, my word!" He continued to rock in his paroxysms of laughter. "And they couldn't touch a girlie or a cash piece. Gawd! what a neat little hell!"

He turned toward his companion.

"And what did you do, you fat, old crook? What did you do? Stay on for a little of the loot the American wouldn't take?"

Colonel Swank resumed his narrative as though there had been no interruption.

"I remained," he said, "though not entirely at my own initiative. The old Viceroy had drawn the conclusion from some remarks of Major Dillard that the white cross which the monks had put up before the gate of the Monastery was a protecting symbol of the great Christian religions, and that in some manner its effect on Major Dillard had produced the result which followed. This impression doubtless arose from the fact that in his order to the Prussian officers Major Dillard had directed that the cross should be permitted to remain. It was his idea doubtless that this religious symbol would help to protect the Monastery from the remainder of the Expeditionary Force. They might take it to be a hospital, or some missionary place of refuge. But the Viceroy got the idea that it was to the sacredness of this symbol that he owed his protection, and he began to inquire of me upon the point. Why was the cross a sacred symbol in our religion?

"I explained it to him: that, Jesus of Nazareth, the Messiah of the Christians, had been crucified on a tree, and that this cross was symbolical of that crucifixion; of that vicarious atonement for the sins of the world. He did not understand the metaphysics of my explanation; but he understood its physical essentials; that the God of the Christians had been crucified on a tree, and that this concrete representation was, therefore, sacred, as the images of Buddha in his eternal calm, with the lotus flower in his hand; that the cross meant to all Western religions what the image of Buddha meant to Asia.

"He understood crucifixion. It was a torture of death known to the Chinese; but reserved only for the lowest criminals. It had been supplanted in later years by the *lingchi*, or death of a thousand cuts; but it was an old practice, and the archives of his province contained ancient paintings of it. He interrogated me minutely upon the details of this crucifixion, and I gave him an accurate picture of it: The Man of Sorrows crowned with thorns, and nailed to the cross. But in the translation I made use always of the Chinese word for tree. A lack of precision in language which had presently a definite result."

Again Bow Bell spat upon the deck.

"The hell you did," he said. "You sanctimonious old crook. You ought to have had your tongue cut out. No missionary society would put up with you for a minute. You used to be a faro dealer in Hongkong until you got too cursed crooked for even a Chinese gambler to stand you."

Colonel Swank did not resent this digression.

"For a week," he said, "I remained in the Monastery as a guest of the Viceroy. I was treated like a prince. I dined on roast quail covered with clotted cream, and candied rose leaves; and then I was given a present for Major Dillard and sent on to the American Division. I traveled in a chair like an envoy, parallel to, but at some distance from, the line of march, and I overtook him before he reached Pekin."

"And what was the present?" said Bow Bell. "Twelve she asses laden with gold?"

"No," replied the Colonel in his weary drawl, "it was not. It was a carving in ivory representing the crucifixion of Jesus of Nazareth as I had described it, wrapped in a piece of black silk embroidered with a white cross, not worth a pound and six pence. The carving, a mediocre work of art, might have been worth a hundred dollars in America.

"You will recall that I used the word tree in my description to the Viceroy, and this carving represented an ivory tree made of the whole segment of an elephant tusk. It was about four inches in diameter, and ten inches high. The base represented the roots of the tree spread out, so that the thing would stand in balance. Broken limbs represented the cross pieces to which the hands of the figure were nailed. The feet were spiked together on the trunk; the head thrown back, and encircled with a crown of thorns, made the entire top of the carving, that is to say, the top of the tree."

"Well, for Gawd's sake," said Bow Bell. "A piece of carved elephant's tusk for a job like that!... Did you steal it?"

Colonel Swank went on:

"And it was carved in tiny English letters around the base with a legend, not badly worded for a pagan imitation of the Scriptures: 'Inasmuch as you turned your head to save us, may He turn His head to save you'.... No, I didn't steal it. How could I steal it? There was a Chinese runner on each side of the chair. I was never out of sight of them, and they each had a knife. I delivered it to the Major."

"Well, he didn't get much for his trouble," said Bow Bell. "It's no good to be good!"

His voice descended into a confidential note; he leaned a little toward his companion.

"Now, you said you had a notion about this thing at the beginning of your talk. What was that notion, Colonel?"

"As I recall," Swank continued, "it was a discourse about the exaggerated value which devotees of a religion place upon their symbols. They all seem to feel that the sacredness of these symbols is an ample payment for any immensity of service. It is a very strange and universal belief. The English resident of a native state in India once received a gold Buddha for saving a Rajah's life, and it was not even gold. It was only plated."

"But that's not all you said," interrupted Bow Bell. "You said you were going to America. You said you were going to find that crucifix. You said you had a notion about it. What is your notion?"

For a moment Colonel Swank did not reply. His hand moved the long sharp blade of the knife peeling off ribbons of pine from the piece of soft wood. The sun was going down, and the sea continued to be as placid as a sheet of glass. There was no one in sight on the rear of the deck of the freighter; but at the moment Swank began to speak one of the Chinese crew appeared. The Colonel lowered his voice, and what he said passed in a whisper to his companion.

What happened after that was fatal and unforeseen for this ill-omened person.

Bow Bell looked quickly about the deck. The individual of the Chinese crew had passed behind the leprous stack of the freighter. Bow Bell spoke softly, and leaned over toward his companion.

"You're going to get a lot of ash on your shirt, Colonel," he said; and taking hold of the hand in which his companion held the knife with which he had been whittling the piece of packing board, he brought it up with a firm grasp, and drove the long blade into the man's chest just under the heart, guiding it carefully with the fingers of his left hand so that the blade would enter in the interstice between the ribs.

For a moment the huge body of the man did not move. Then, his eyes widened, and his mouth extended in a sort of wonder.

"Why, you dirty little beast!" he drawled. "You dirty little beast!"

Then his head fell forward, the great, slack body quivered, shuddered, and was motionless.

Bow Bell turned the handle of the knife down, pressed the blade in against the chest to prevent hemorrhage, buttoned the frock coat over the knife, tucked the disturbed, cotton handkerchief into the man's collar: And to the eye, Colonel Swank, drunk with opium, had fallen asleep over his narrative, his chin sunk comfortably on his chest, the body propped against the drum, and supported by Bow Bell's shoulder.

A moment later the Chinese deck hand came out from behind the stack, and moved along the rail of the rear deck, making his inspection of the ship. And the iron nerve of Bow Bell presented itself.

"Hey, John," he said. "Speakee Linglish?"

"Vellee good," replied the Chinaman, continuing to move along the rail. "Speakum Plittsburg: Hullee-lup, hullee-lup, lu lalle—bastard!—Speakum Hongkong pololo plony belong-house." His voice, went suddenly up in a high, sharp, whining cry: "Lide 'im off, Major. Oh, damn!"

Then he shuffled off unconcernedly along the rail around the rear of the ship, and disappeared toward the prow.

Night descended.

A little later Bow Bell lifted the apparently opium-drunken body of Colonel Swank to his feet, and helped him to the rail of the ship. There the two stood for a moment close together as in confidential talk, until, as the gunman turned away, the opium-drunken Colonel, by some loss of balance, fell forward over the rail into the sea.

With a great cry Bow Bell ran forward to report the accident.

* * * *

It was midnight when Marion Dillard returned.

Despair like an opiate had finally drugged her into a sort of physical submission, and she had turned back to the comfort of her house as one on his way to death warms himself before a fire. She let herself in.

The house was silent. The servants, pleased to obtain a holiday on this night, had gone out. She removed her coat and hat, and laid them on a console in the hall; and went into the library. She moved softly, as one will under a breaking mental tension. It was midnight; the great clocks of the city were beginning to strike.

The door to the library was open. Marion Dillard turned from the hall into the room; but on the threshold she stopped. The figure of a man leaned over the library table, a cap pulled over his eyes, a dark handkerchief tied around the lower part of his face. He held the massive, carved ivory crucifix in his hands, and he was intent on some undertaking with it.

The girl took a step forward, and, at the sound, the figure turned, and a weapon flashed in his hand. Immediately the silence in the room was shattered by the explosion of a shot. Marion Dillard imagined that the burglar had fired at her; but, if so, why did the creature sway, put out a convulsive hand, drop his weapon on the rug, and crumple in a heap.

The voice of the detective, whom she had found on guard at the gate as she went out gave the explanation. Walker came forward from behind the curtain of a window.

"Bad gunman," he said, "wanted all over the world. I had to kill him."

And he indicated the crumpled body of Mr. Bow Bell.

"But what was he doing to that ivory crucifix? It looked like he was trying to twist it."

Marion Dillard went forward and took up the heavy piece of carved ivory.

The head thrown back crowned with thorns, making the top of the tree on which the figure was impaled, had been twisted around until it faced backward. It was loose, and she lifted the head out of the carving.

The whole interior of the ivory tree was hollow, and packed with rice powder.

The girl picked up a metal paper knife, and loosened the powder in the hollow ivory. Hard pellets were embedded in the rice powder, and when she released them, great oriental pearls appeared—huge, magnificent—a double handful of them; unequaled, matchless, priceless, worth the ransom of a province.

And at the moment, the last stroke of the clocks sounded above the city, commemorating the hour of the birth of the Saviour of the World.